C000104479

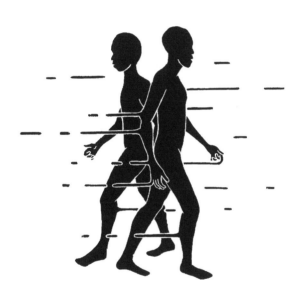

Copyright © 2021 by Robert Pantano

All rights reserved. No part of this publication may be reproduced, distributed, or transmitted in any form or by any means, including photocopying, recording, or other electronic or mechanical methods, without permission in writing from the publisher, except in the case of brief quotes used in reviews and other non-commercial purposes permitted by copyright law.

The characters and events in this book are fictitious. Any apparent similarities to actual persons or events, living or dead, past or present, are not intended by the author and is entirely coincidental.

A Pursuit of Wonder publication.

Contents

Preface

This book contains a collection of short stories originally published as videos between 2018 and 2020 on the author's YouTube channel Pursuit of Wonder. The stories have since been re-edited and improved but broadly remain consistent.

The original videos can still be found on the Pursuit of Wonder YouTube channel at the time of this publication.

The Nova Effect – The Tragedy of Good Luck

A man named Eric is on a walk with his dog, Nova. While on the walk, Eric loses Nova after she pulls the leash from his hand in pursuit of a rabbit that happens to jump out of a bush as they pass by it. Eric chases after Nova, but this only inspires her to run faster until she completely eludes Eric's vision, continuing on her pursuit of the rabbit that has, by now, hidden somewhere in the other direction. After several hours pass, it becomes clear that Nova has outrun her sense of orientation and is now lost.

Eric spends the rest of the day and the days following searching for Nova. He also notifies neighbors, enlists friends and family to help, and puts up signs.

A week goes by, and Nova is still missing. Eric is devastated beyond comprehension. He thinks about how horribly unlucky it was that the rabbit jumped out at just the wrong time and that his hand position was just in the wrong place to allow Nova to pull the leash from it.

A week later, a woman shows up at Eric's front door. She has Nova. After Nova and Eric reconnect in a chaotic, heartwarming display of affection, Eric thanks the woman. She introduces herself and tells Eric her name is Vanessa. She's beautiful and about Eric's age. Eric and Vanessa talk for a little while and seem to hit it off. In the following weeks, they hang out several times, and things go so well, they soon begin dating. Eric finds her to be absolutely gorgeous, kind, funny, smart, spontaneous, all the right buzzwords for a perfect romantic partner in a story.

Soon, Eric and Vanessa fall in love. The relationship is everything one could reasonably hope a relationship to be.

Eric thinks about how lucky it was that Vanessa was the person who happened to be in the right place at the right time to find and return Nova.

A couple of months go by. Eric is driving, on his way to pick up Vanessa. While driving through an intersection, Eric is T-boned at full speed by a driver coming from the perpendicular side street who distractedly runs a red light. Eric is knocked unconscious as he and his car are sent in a thrashing 1080-degree spin.

An hour or so later, Eric finds himself in a hospital. A doctor informs Eric of what has happened and explains that he has suffered a severe head injury and that they will need to run some immediate tests as well as a brain scan to determine the severity and if there's any chance of permanent brain damage or internal bleeding.

As his consciousness begins to return to him, Eric thinks about how unlucky he was to have been going to get Vanessa in that exact direction at that exact time. He's furious at the possibility that his life might be ruined because of this one random happenstance.

Eric is held overnight at the hospital. The next day, the doctor comes in to Eric's room. "Eric, how are we doing?" the doctor asks.

"Fine. A little fuzzy I guess," Eric replies.

"Yeah, I would certainly imagine. You took quite the smack," the doctor says.

"Yeah," Eric responds.

"So, I've reviewed the CT scan, and I have some bad news. But I also have some good news."

Confused, Eric says, "Okay, um, I guess I'll take the bad news first."

"Well, technically, they're the same piece of news," says the doctor.

"What do you mean?" Eric asks with an escalating level of concern and confusion.

"The bad news is that we found what appears to be a glioma in your brain." The doctor pauses for a moment as Eric looks at him, unaware of what this means. "It's a tumor," the doctor continues. "The good news, though, is we found what appears to be a glioma in your brain."

"What do you mean? How is that good news?" Eric asks.

"This tumor has nothing to do with your accident. You actually got out of the accident relatively unharmed. But because of your accident, we ran the brain scan. Because of the brain scan, we found the tumor. Normally, we only catch a tumor like this after someone realizes something's wrong when they start to feel the symptoms, which is almost always too late. Because we found the tumor right now, though, we caught it while it's still benign, before it became malignant and grew into any other areas of your brain, which in almost all cases becomes fatal. Since it's still in this stage, though, we should be able to remove it almost entirely without any issue. Eric, in a weird way, this car accident basically saved your life. So, you see, it's sort of good news disguised as bad news," the doctor concludes.

Eric starts to feel a weird, visceral tingling sensation and becomes slightly disoriented. Maybe it's the head injury. Maybe it's the emotion of the situation. Maybe it's the fact that the doctor just essentially said the same thing twice, but Eric experienced two totally different mental responses. Maybe it's everything. He looks around the room. He thinks about how lucky he was to have been going to get Vanessa, in that exact direction at that exact time. He thinks about how lucky he was to have gotten in the car accident. He thinks about how weird it is to think this—for something so bad to be so good and for something so good to be so bad. In this moment, Eric realizes how little he knows about what anything actually is. That he has never and can never know what exists on the other side of anything that happens to him or because of him, no matter how good or bad, lucky or unlucky any of it might seem. Eric feels a strange, paradoxical sense of helplessness and liberation.

About a week later, Eric undergoes brain surgery to remove the tumor. The surgery is successful. Eric is mostly as good as new, with exception to a scar running down the side of his scalp.

Several days later, after being released from the hospital, Eric is recovering at home with Vanessa. To get some fresh air, he takes Nova out for a walk.

The Beginning & End of Humanity

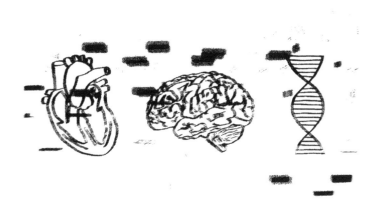

The year is 1968. A seven-year-old boy named Clay has just finished building a contraption that remotely opens and closes a little exterior door for his family's dog. He is constantly building toys and mechanical contraptions like this one, using spare bike parts, old TVs, radios, and any other objects he can get his hands on.

Eight years later. The year is 1976. The first personal computers hit the market. Clay, now fifteen, finds himself immediately drawn to the newly developing computer industry. He soon begins creating software programs and has a unique way of understanding how technology and humans can interact. Throughout his adolescence, because of this interest, understanding, and his natural ingenuity, Clay creates and sells several computer programs, develops a software business, appears on TV about a dozen times, meets the president, and graduates from MIT.

The year is 1982. Clay is twenty-one. Clay loses his mother to coronary heart disease. Without ever having a father in the picture, Clay's mother was one of the few people he truly loved and could count on in his life. Clay struggles with his mother's death. The experience and idea of her death, and death in general, makes no sense to him. Clay wonders why a conscious, intelligent being, unlike any other species, dies like every other species. How can a species that can create fire, tools, computers, airplanes, rockets, medicine, and so on, still die, basically the same as a slug or a lizard?

Early on, Clay forms the belief that it doesn't have to be this way. He believes that in the near future, humanity can overcome the dependence on its weak and entropic biological body through technology.

Clay embarks on his pursuit of this belief. He studies and develops his theories and begins to immerse himself further and further into the newly emerging computer software and biotechnologies.

The year is 1997. At age thirty-six, Clay starts a biotech company named Kurve, which creates algorithms and computer models related to human biology and genetics. Clay soon discovers that the brain is quite similar to the software he's creating to study the brain. The brain recognizes patterns, organizes these patterns hierarchically, and is then able to formulate an awareness of its conditions and make judgments accordingly, just like the newly developing artificial intelligence software Clay is working with. In this, Clay realizes that if the structure of human consciousness can be fully modeled and replicated, it could also be, theoretically, placed onto any device of replicable function and sustained indefinitely. In other words, the human experience of self could essentially be limitless beyond the human body.

Thirty-two years later, the year is 2029. At age sixty-eight, Clay and his biotech company successfully reverse engineer the entire function of the human brain. This, in combination with a vast array of other innovations in the biotechnology space, now means that human consciousness can be enhanced, maintained, and transferred through and onto any hardware device or cloud service entity. People now have the opportunity to think and understand at a rate that is exponentially greater than any conceived possibility of the past. Mental conditions are now able to be modified beyond inherited genetics. Lifelong mental disorders can be eradicated. Bacterial and age-related diseases can be circumvented.

Eight years later, Clay is seventy-six. The year is 2037. Clay is the first person to successfully upload his entire brain function to an outside, hybrid entity. Now, at any point, Clay can change over to a separate, synthetic body and reconnect to his consciousness via a software access server, like the cloud, and still maintain his sense of self. With this, Clay would lead humanity into a new realm of existence: a life of boundless consciousness.

The year is 2486. Clay, along with the rest of humanity, lives hundreds of years past the previously standard life expectancy. Clay travels the whole world and visits everyplace there is to see. He reads every book, sees every movie, watches every video, visits every website, masters every language, hears every story, and learns every skill. He falls in to love and out of love, over and over. Hundreds of years turn to thousands. Thousands turn to millions. The year becomes irrelevant. Every time boredom, overpopulation, or overconsumption appear to be on the horizon, new worlds are discovered and created.

Clay explores new planets, new galaxies, new dimensions. He meets new beings from other worlds. New realms of art, science, and entertainment emerge and die, emerge and die. He experiences new types of feelings, new ways of thinking, new ways of experiencing.

Millions and millions more years go by. Clay's home, his mother, his sister, his dog, his childhood, his mortal self, the conditions of the world he was born in, have all long been forgotten, stored away like an old file on an old hard drive he forgot he ever had. Clay continues on for millions of years. He explores more worlds and more realms of life, on and on, until eventually the stars begin to die, the galaxies begin to dissolve, and the universe begins to burn out.

Clay accomplished what had been but a fantasy for all of human history before him—supremacy over one's nature. Immortality. He traveled the cosmos. He made millions and millions of discoveries. He learned everything there was to know, every law of physics, every rule of reality, all to end up here, about to die with everything else. *What was it all for?* Clay wonders to himself. What was the point of beating his own death, only to be subjected to the death of the universe? How could a species that transcended its own biology and the nature of life itself just die off with the universe like all the other little particles and amoebas that came before it?

In the remaining moments of the smothering universe, Clay decides to create one last thing. Now, having learned all the mechanics of nature and how the universe works, Clay begins to construct a blueprint for a new one. Like creating the rules of a video game, he renders the code for a new universe. He makes it hard, but not impossible. Long but not without end. He makes it so each level gets a little more complex, yet a little more interesting. A little more daunting, yet a little more rewarding. He makes it so the rules of the universe change a little over time, never too far so it makes no sense, but never too close that it makes complete sense. He hides the endgame so far from the starting point, only in the final stage can it be seen and comprehended. He conceals the truths amidst the chaos. The logic amidst the disorder. The meaning amidst the lack thereof. Finally, he leaves the possibility for creating anew. Clay finishes. "It's perfect," he says to himself.

The universe begins to compress tighter and tighter. The dying energy dries out any remaining life. The last stars turn off. The last planets explode. Everything gives one last nod of farewell to this existence as it squeezes back into nothingness. As the energy tightens into a final pinpoint, Clay's new universe explodes. A bursting of color, matter, and energy floods out, reversing the nothing into an ever-expanding everything. Time and space begin again. Stars fill the sky. Celestial collisions occur. Planets form. Bacteria and amoebas flow around each other. Life emerges. A trial-and-error of existence unfolds. A sequence of living and dying, trying and failing, evolving and adapting, thinking and talking, building and creating.

Years and years and years would go by. The year is 1968. A seven-year-old boy named Clay has just finished building a contraption that remotely opens and closes a little exterior door for his family's dog. He is constantly building toys and mechanical contraptions like this one, using spare bike parts, old TVs, radios, and any other objects he can get his hands on. He'll probably do a lot in this life.

As Clay finishes the dog's door, his sister asks him, "Didn't you already make that?"

"Yeah. I just took it apart and made it again," replies Clay.

"Why?" asks his sister.

"I don't know. It was fun, and I wanted to see if I could make it better," replies Clay.

"Well, is it better now?" asks his sister.

Clay replies, "No. It was fine."

The Feeling That Life Will Never Be as Good as It Once Was

A young girl named Sarah got ready for her first day of fifth grade. Having moved over the summer, she was now at a new school in a new town. Naturally, she was scared and nervous about what it would be like and if she would be liked. Before leaving for school, she sat at the kitchen table, enjoying her favorite cartoon and eating her favorite cereal. About two hours later, she was at school, lost and nervous.

As the first school day turned into the first school week, first month, and first half of the year, Sarah remained fairly nervous each day. Every day felt like a minefield of social games and classroom stresses. She worried about boys, and she worried about the popular girls who weren't very friendly to her. She wasn't bullied, per se, but she often felt inferior and uncomfortable. About halfway through the year, though, Sarah started to form a nice little friend group of other kids dealing with similar things, which helped. One of the few things that helped her get through each week, after morning cartoons and cereal, was recess with her friends. They wouldn't need to do too much–just hang out, joke freely, swing on the swings, and flirt with each other. The whole world became an elementary school playground as everything else dissolved outside the fence of the schoolyard.

Every Monday, Sarah had a math test after recess, which always kind of ruined the day for her. She struggled with math and always felt stupid during the tests. Every Wednesday and Friday, she also had to give presentations in two classes, which she also hated. Just in general, she felt more stressed that year than any previous school years, and every day was an uphill battle.

One day, after a math test, Sarah left class to go to get a drink of water. On her way to the water fountain, she noticed a second or third grader crying in the hallway with a guidance counselor. The counselor was saying, "It's okay. It's just a game. It's just a game," over and over. As Sarah walked past them, she thought to herself how little kids have no idea how good they have it.

Six years later, Sarah was sixteen and a junior in high school. It had been one of her hardest school years yet. She struggled to keep her grades up and felt the pressure of needing to do so more than ever. For the first time, she started looking at colleges and having to think about her life after school. All of it terrified and stressed her out.

That same year, Sarah got her license and could essentially go wherever she wanted. She had to schedule around when her older brother was using the family's second car, though, which meant she and her brother fought over it nearly every time. When she did get to use it, Sarah and her friends would go out and enjoy the new sense of freedom that came with being that age. They would go to the park, the mall, parties, each other's houses, and sometimes just drive around and smoke weed and get food. Most of the time, it was really fun, but a lot of the times, Sarah felt a weird increasing amount of competitiveness with her friends, especially when boys were around. One boy in particular, who Sarah liked a lot, ended up making out with one of her friends when they were at the mall together. Of course, this devastated Sarah, and she rushed off and sat in the food court by herself, trying not to cry while she waited for her mom to come pick her up–to avoid going home with her friends. While she sat there, thinking about how horrible the year had been with all the stresses of school and new responsibilities and increasing social challenges, a group of three little girls, who looked to be around fifth or sixth graders, walked by her and sat a table just a couple of feet away. Sarah overheard them complaining about a teacher or something, and she condescendingly laughed to herself. She thought about how they had no idea how easy they had it.

Simultaneously, she was reminded of her own elementary and middle school years. She remembered how easy and fun it was to be at an age when you still had things like recess; just hanging out, flirting with boys with no real pressure, and no real-life stresses other than silly little tests and other dumb little kids. She got images in her head of her fifth- and sixth-grade classrooms and hallways, recalling various specific memories that she had forgotten about but were now suddenly being played out of the strange storage center of the brain like blurry little movies. In that moment, she felt a longing to be back there.

Eight more years went by. Sarah was twenty-four, living in New York City after having gone to college in Syracuse, New York, several hundred miles away from home. She decided to stay in New York after graduating and moved to the city for work. She was living in an apartment that she split with four other people. It was tight quarters, but the group had become like a little family, and something was always going on in the apartment. The whole group would sometimes go out to the bars and clubs together, bringing their other friend groups all into one big one. However, a good percentage of the time, most of her friends and roommates were busy, tired, or uninterested in going out, all with their own lives, relationships, job schedules, and so on.

During this time, despite living with four people, Sarah constantly felt lonely. It had been three years since she broke up with a guy she had dated seriously in college, because he drank all the time and was an asshole when he did. But she still wasn't really over him, and she definitely wasn't over being alone.

For work during this time, she was a typesetter for a midsize publishing company, helping create text layouts for business-oriented books and print publications. The job was both tedious and stressful.

The pressure of the work environment paired with her lack of personal connection to the outcome made it meaninglessly difficult. She loved living in New York City, though, and her work options were limited in order to afford the nearly impossible cost to stay. In order to try to increase her income, ever since graduating college, she had been trying to build up her own graphic design business on the side, which she put most of her spare time toward. She was always looking for freelance projects and working on personal portfolio pieces. But she had yet to find any real success. She worried deeply about the direction of her life, or lack thereof, and felt aimless, incapable, and afraid of never finding success in anything personally meaningful. The unknown and uncertainty gnawed at her like a cramped muscle in her spine.

One night, on a fairly ordinary Saturday, Sarah drank wine by herself in her apartment while working on a graphic design piece. A couple of hours in, she was properly drunk. While looking for source material and old files, she found herself looking at old photos on her laptop. Specifically, photos of her and her ex-boyfriend in college. This then led her to look at other old photos and videos from college and high school: parties, projects, travels, dorms, her winter and summer breaks, videos that she and her friends made at sleepovers, and so on. She thought about how fun college was and how easy high school was. How nice it was to have friends who weren't always busy, to have fun just driving around and going to the mall, to not have to worry about real money problems, to have summers that still felt like summers, to have semesters that ended and began, to just be a student with nothing that serious on her plate, and to still have a boyfriend who made her loneliness feel less real. In this moment, Sarah felt a deep, nostalgic longing to be back in the time of those photos.

Twenty-one years went by. Sarah was forty-four and had become a wife; a successful, independent graphic designer; and the mother of two boys. When she was thirty-six, one of her designs that she posted on the internet got noticed by the founder of a startup tech company. The founder liked it so much, she reached out and asked Sarah if the company could purchase an iteration of the design and use it as their logo. Sarah, of course, agreed, and two years later, after the company had become a massive success, she was given the opportunity to lead the company's brand identity, icon designs, and nearly all other visual elements. Ever since, Sarah slowly became a highly sought-after, world-renowned graphic designer, eventually starting her own studio and design consulting agency, partnering with several other industry leaders. Between this and her two children, almost every week was filled to capacity. There was never a dull moment, which was engaging, but also absolutely exhausting. She appreciated her job and loved her family, but Sarah often found herself feeling suffocated by her life–not just by the intense stress, pressure, or responsibility of everything, but by the feeling that all possibilities for anything else were essentially gone forever.

One Friday, Sarah picked up her youngest son from baseball practice in between two of her afternoon meetings. On the way back to the office, after dropping her son off at home, she stopped for a drink at a local bar to give herself a moment to breathe. She had two more meetings that day and then a seminar presentation that night, along with two more big presentations over the weekend. This was a lot, but normal for her. While at the bar, a small group of twenty- or thirty-something-year-olds came in and sat near her. They were talking about what sounded like a business they were working on or toward. Sarah listened while she drank. She looked over out of the corner of her eye and thought about how nice it would be to be that age again, to still have a friend group like that, to be able to go out once or twice a weekend with no worries, or to even just be able to stay in by herself and drink wine, relax, and work on her own projects with no distractions. She remembered the times when she was first living in the city: the shitty apartments that she loved, the roommates who were always around to have fun, the nights out, being young and single. She thought back to how exciting it was to be in the face of the unknown. Everything in her life now was mostly figured out. And now, she longed to be back when nothing was figured out and everything was still possible. She thought to herself, almost slightly mad at the naïve young adults next to her, that twenty-year-olds never realize how good they have it.

The next forty years went by. Sarah was eighty-four. She had developed moderate osteoporosis, which had begun to somewhat limit her mobility, with all likelihood of worsening. She lived in an assisted living center for elderly individuals with memory and mobility issues.

On a normal Sunday, her sixteen-year-old granddaughter, Olivia, visited her. Sarah and her granddaughter were very close, and Olivia would often visit to talk, keep her company, and ask her for advice. On this particular day, the two watched a movie together. It was a sad movie where someone died really young from cancer. When the movie was over, the two cried a little while they talked about it. At one point while talking about life and aging, Olivia asked Sarah if she regretted anything. Sarah thought for a moment about how honest she wanted to be with Olivia. Then she answered and said that one of the things she regretted is that she never realized how good she had it until it was too late, until she was this frail, old woman, alone in an assisted living home with nothing to do. She said that she would give anything to be back any age younger than seventy, not even to do anything different, but to just do it again. She explained how she wished she could be forty-five again and be passionate and engaged in a job she thrived in, to still be a wife and a mother of little children, to still be front and center of the orchestra of her life.

Sarah ended by saying, "Don't overlook what you have while you have it, Olivia. You don't realize how good it is to be where you are until you aren't. And you don't realize how young you are until you realize you were just young for the last time ever. Don't wait until you're my age. It's no fun." After asking a few more questions, the two said goodbye with a hug, and Olivia went home, leaving Sarah alone in her room. Before turning the TV back on, Sarah thought about her own advice for a moment. She wasn't sure if she meant what she said or if it was more of just what she thought she was supposed to say if she was in a movie or a story or something. She thought about how she was essentially saying that life comes down to being this old, and everything before it was good, and everything after it is basically the runoff. But then this made her think about how even there, she wasn't listening to her own advice.

She considered how, in that moment, she was, in fact, existing in yet another period of her life that, if she lived longer, she would almost certainly look back fondly on; if in ten years, she was still alive but completely bedridden or beginning to lose her mind, she would look back at this time when she still had a body and brain that worked, a time when she had essentially nothing to worry about other than what activities she wanted to do at the home, a time when her kids and grandkids visited her, and she still knew who they were, and she would long to be back.

This then made Sarah question how she looked at her whole life, during each moment. She always knew that she looked at the past through rose-colored glasses. She knew everyone did and that this was just something written into the script of life. But she never really thought about what this meant about the present: that if seemingly every version of the past could be viewed through the positive color of rose, then that same shade of rose must exist in every moment and period of life–including this one. And that perhaps the problem is, rose is just one shade of many colors that coat every moment at the same time. And when you mix multiple primary and complementary colors together, you get a brownish or grayish color. And when you see a brown or gray, it's essentially impossible to see the other shades of colors that helped make it.

Sarah realized in this, that even in the mostly positive, rose-colored moments of life, it didn't take much green or yellow to make everything look brown. And when reflecting back, she didn't see the other colors of anxiety or stress, not because they didn't exist, but because the stressful, confusing, and overwhelming parts of her memories weren't so stressful, confusing, and overwhelming anymore, now that she knew how they were all resolved or no longer relevant. The complementary colors dissolved away and left the primary memory in it of itself, free from all the moods that painted over the experience while she was experiencing it. But the rose was always there, somewhere. And in this moment, Sarah finally saw it while she was in it.

Birth – The Biggest Choice You Didn't Make

It is sometime in the distant future. Your consciousness has been digitally linked and integrated into a brain machine interface located inside an orblike spacecraft that was launched from the dying planet of your origins. Like all things, your planet reached its final moments as its lonely star began to run out of fuel, ceasing all thermonuclear reactions and growing into a red giant on the way to its final ember, slowly engulfing your planet in the process. In an act of desperation, you and many others launched yourself into deep space in an unlikely search for another planet that can sustain life on its own.

Like a school of minnows, you swim through the sea of space, each in individual spacecrafts, all coordinated together as well as you can. Inside your spacecraft, your body is held in a cryogenic stasis tube. It will last indefinitely throughout the journey. Your spacecraft, however, will not. Sustained by a circulatory process of dark matter collection, your fuel source is essentially endless, but your spacecraft will face its inevitable demise through erosion or malfunction. It cannot endlessly sustain the chaos that is the universe or the entropy that inhabits everything inside it. If you do not find a planet in time that is, at a minimum, tolerable to life, you will never be able to exist as a body with a home, and the timeline of your life will end with the spacecraft's.

Even with no guarantee of a future, even with being presented with such a horrible circumstance, at this moment, one could argue that you are unfathomably lucky. There were billions of others left behind who died with the planet, all for horrible reasons that no one deserved any more or less than you deserved to be one of the ones who was launched. And beyond that, among the billions that were, you are of the small percentage who made it past the initial launch. Hundreds of millions of others combusted in the process of the launch or met their demise early on in the journey thereafter as a result of collisions with space debris, spacecraft malfunctions, falling off course, or any of the other unfortunate possibilities. By the luck of luck itself, in total, the odds of you making it even this far were something around one in four hundred trillion. And now, you continue onward into the unknown.

Your spacecraft hurtles through the galaxy, equipped with a plethora of technologies that assist you in the mission of locating a new planet that needs only one thing: just the right mix of everything.

In between intermittent periods of extended sleep and autopilot modes, using your thoughts alone, you monitor your journey through the spacecraft's navigation system. You do your best looking for galactic habitable zones. In the entire galaxy, at best, only about 10 percent makes up what could be considered these zones. And areas within these zones that contain stars suitable for livable planetary conditions could be closer to less than just 1 percent of the entire galaxy. At the most optimistic of estimations, odds are less than one in a million of finding a planet that is tolerable to life, let alone cordial. And that's not even accounting for any other factors that might happen to you along the way. For this whole thing to be successful, in total from start to finish, your odds would likely end up being somewhere between one in four hundred quadrillion and impossible. To even have any odds at all at this point is a miracle of odds itself.

As you continue to pass cold, dry, barren planets, all uninhabit-

THE HIDDEN STORY OF EVERY PERSON

able to you, you lose more and more hope. Without giving up entirely, you return to a long, group-coordinated, auto-piloted slumber.

After some unimaginable length of time, suddenly, the interface awakes you. It has, for the first time since being launched, detected a planet that seems to show signs of potential inhabitability. You and the lonely remaining survivors move forth toward the planet in elated awe over this impossible discovery.

As you approach, the interface retrieves imagery and data, revealing a planet that seems to have just the right mass for just the right force of gravity to keep you on it, while allowing you to still move; just the right mix of atmospheric conditions for just the right mix of molecules to form and sustain themselves as water and oxygen; just the right mix of warm and cold temperatures, never being too much of either; just the right proximity to the nearest star for light and energy to fuel just the right rhythmic order of continued motion; all just right to allow nutrients to grow from the planet's surface and for life to live.

As you approach even closer, the interface is able to scan and interpret more imagery and data, revealing what looks to be a species of beings that look just like you, as if they are fundamentally no different from you at all. In this moment, you realize that not only are you going to be able to live a life in your body, but against almost all conceivable odds, you happened across what seems like a planet that is almost perfect for it. A planet with sunsets and ponds and oceans and trees and food and life—all shared with others like you. The luck is beyond absurd. Beyond the mere concept of absurd. And yet, here you are.

You continue closer and closer, overjoyed and anticipating your arrival. Before you get too close, though, you probe the entire planet one more time, and all of a sudden, the interface reveals footage of a previously unseen horror that awaits you. It shows you a misery that exists on the planet that you will almost certainly have to assume. It shows you disease and bacteria and germs that cover the planet, almost all of which you will be at risk of becoming infected by. It shows that in many of those beings that look just like you, that you will inexorably be a part of, exists a malevolence, a greed, a violence, a potential hatred. It shows you the horrible storms and tragedies and disasters that the planet experiences with no real warning and nothing much to do about any of it. The planet is at least equally terrifying and horrible as it is perfect and beautiful. But by the same token, it is equally perfect and beautiful as it is terrifying and horrible.

In this moment, you are confronted with a choice: to land or not to land?

You consider how, with as far as certainty can be certain, this is your only hope at life. And against all possible odds, you are here—at this distant, solitary planet amidst the cold dark of a seemingly unending, lifeless universe. And with every incoming ship, including your own, there is the potential to bring to the planet a compassion and love and the same unbelievably favorable odds of hope that got you here in the first place.

You make what you believe is the obvious choice.

The Art of Loneliness

We got a new guy a couple months ago. Not just a new guy, but a first-timer. It's always interesting getting a new guy because you can sort of see yourself in them and vicariously experience when you first got sent in here without actually needing to experience it for yourself again. You wouldn't think you would want to even vicariously do that, considering how surface-level horrible the experience is, but there's always something appealing about it. It's a reminder of how far you've come, I suppose.

When he first came in, you could see it on his face. The same look every guy has when they enter into this new world for the first time. It's an awareness of uncertainty paired with a refusal to accept it. Fear masked by bravado. The kind of bravado that needs bravado to prove itself; the self-announcing sort, which is almost always a surefire sign that there exists a fear in the person that they haven't even yet braved confronting. It was carried in the way he walked and talked. He was still hopeful that he could force his way through the whole thing. He was still hopeful that it wouldn't be what he knew, deep down, it would. New guys always do this. I did it.

The first day is the worst. And then the next several dozens of days after aren't really that much better. You exist in a weird state of limbo for a while, while you go through the process of denial. Not even just conscious denial, but a natural resistance to your new circumstances. The first weeks and sometimes the first months are just a transitioning period where your mind seems to have a lag time behind reality. For a while, you are literally in this new world, but all your senses and expectations are still in the old. And in this, you find yourself searching for something that doesn't exist anymore, fighting against the nothingness met by your expectations.

This is the hardest part—coming to terms with the change. And until you've come to terms with being isolated and confined from your previous world, you definitely haven't come anywhere close to figuring out how to be okay with it. Eventually, though, you do. And for some, you even come to like it. But first, for most people, including myself, as the initial days start to flip into weeks and months, you seem to dip, for at least some period of time, into hopelessness. It seems, for some reason, you have to go there first, as if hopelessness is always on the way between two different states of hopefulness, and it's the only way through to other side.

I think anytime you're confronted with how little control you have, how cruel everything (including yourself) can be, how easily everything can be taken away or flipped on its head, and how truly helpless, dissolute, and alone you are, the only way to keep hope is to quickly touch hopelessness first and feel how bad it hurts. It's like a little kid touching a hot stove or lightbulb. You almost don't believe it's that bad. Or for some reason, you're just curious about how bad it really is, and you have to touch it to believe it. Once you have, though, you're pretty much ready to take your hand off as soon as possible and find some other way to live. That's how it was for me at least. Some people do seem to get stuck there, though. Sadly. Some people like the additional pain.

Even after it had been two or three weeks since the new guy got here, he was still antsy every day, all day—causing fights, acting strange, forcing himself into this and that. Even when he was physically doing nothing, you could see him racing around in his head,

THE HIDDEN STORY OF EVERY PERSON

anxious and guilty of his procrastination with reality.

In truth, you're always isolated in yourself in your own isolated section of the universe, but in here, you feel it both metaphysically and physically. And I think that's why it's so much harder to confront. But equally essential.

It took me a couple of months to properly get past it myself. Eventually, though, you don't have a choice. You either go mad fighting your present reality or you face it. And then, eventually, you wake up, and what once felt completely foreign feels completely normal. And you almost never even notice. Everything becomes a different normal than the normal before, but it feels no less normal. That's the interesting part about normal, that it's essentially always the same no matter what form it takes. As soon as something becomes normal, it feels the same as any other normal. Normal is just normal. Life can somehow be entirely different, and yet it will likely, at some point, feel mostly the same.

I once read that after every seven years or so, every cell in the human body has completely regenerated, and the body becomes made entirely of a different collection of physical material. At which point, nothing that was once *you* is *you* anymore. And across seven years, your life circumstances are likely different too, if not completely different. Meaning both your interior physical state and exterior circumstances are constantly changing completely, and yet you always feel mostly the same. At least in the sense that you still feel like you. It seems as if all processes of change in life are sifted through the same colander of self, and the only thing that is ever consistent on any level in any circumstance is that thing inside your head that continually identifies you with you, despite what's going on around and through it. And that's ultimately what it all comes down to, I think—how well you exist with that strange, central *you* that observes all the other dynamic and constantly changing *yous*. If anything, it is this that solitude and separation provides. The value and reformative nature of confinement is, at least for me, not necessarily to develop into a different person, but to properly face the strange, painful, difficult, and almost inexplicable person you might really be. The person who isn't even really a person, but the thing that lacks a complete and obvious person, but longs relentlessly for one. The truth of what you might be, that you went to great, massive efforts to otherwise avoid. And instead, you direct your efforts to learn how to live with this, rather than always lashing and flailing away from it.

That's where the real trouble came from, for me anyway. Eventually, if your strategy is to flail violently against yourself in an effort to overtake it, you'll end up going to the end of the world, losing everything you have and love, just to ultimately end up being put here to confront the same fact that you knew all along: that you always go with you.

Arguably, some level of solitude is inevitable in any life. But perhaps some level of deeper intentional solitude is necessary for a good one. At least for a period of time.

Even in a crowd of thousands of people, every person is ultimately alone inside their head, a solitary receiver of everything. Everything and everyone is experienced individually, skull by skull, moment by moment, once, for all eternity. And so, what does it mean to be a solitary receiver of a world of noise if, when the noise is turned down, you can't barely stand it? Perhaps some decent amount of solitude grants you the first step in confronting just how broken the receiver inherently is, finally letting you hear the static buzz that's been humming in the background of everything, that you can only really notice when nearly everything else turns down. At first, this humming drove me crazy, sometimes to the brink of all hopelessness, but then, like everything else, you begin to adapt. You begin to better accept it, learn how to live with it, and use it properly, now that you know what's been there causing most of the problems.

Granted, this is all just my experience, and I don't wish to portray it as anything but that. Nor do I wish to portray any conclusive awareness as to how I might turn out and what this all might equate to when my term is over, and I'm finally released back into the world. I think it probably takes a full lifetime to ever know what you really are and what good anything was for you. But if there's any hope in ever being okay in any version of life, despite this—any hope in ever

THE HIDDEN STORY OF EVERY PERSON

feeling like one has any level of agency over themselves while in the chaos of the outside world—I think one must first be able to feel okay and in control of themselves when nearly all other factors of distractions have been subtracted, and your freedom and sense of life has been narrowed all the way down to your skull-sized domain.

I know everyone in here doesn't have the luxury of hope, but for those who do, I think it would only be but another crime to squander it.

And I was happy to see that after about three or four months in, the new guy chilled out. He stopped causing fights, stopped acting crazy. It's mostly always the same. Eventually, everyone figures out how to be okay. Eventually, you don't have a choice.

The False Memory Effect

A man named Charlie stands on a stage in front of a crowd of a few thousand people. He is receiving an Oscar for Best Director. Filled with nerves, pride, and a mix of other unfamiliar emotions, he looks out at the crowd as they cheer for him. The cheer fades as he begins to speak. "Thank you. Wow. Um. First of all, I want to thank my mother and father for their support through everything. I want to thank my wife, Kara, and my daughter, Olivia, for the light and inspiration you guys bring to my life." Charlie pauses for a second and looks down, flustered by the pressure to remember everything he wants to say. He quickly recovers and picks back up. "I want to thank the entire cast and crew. You guys truly brought this film to life and made it special, and I couldn't have done it without each and every one of you. Lastly, I want to thank my longtime collaborator and best friend, Nick. I believe we were just eight or nine when we made our first film together ... and if I remember correctly, all things considered, it was pretty good."

Nick, sitting in the front section of the crowd, also nominated for an Oscar, smiles and laughs as he lightly points his finger at Charlie in a gesture of camaraderie.

"I'll never forget that experience," Charlie continues. "It changed my life forever. And now, here I am living out the childhood dream that formed that day, and I couldn't be more grateful." Charlie nods, says thank you one last time, and holds up his award, giving it a little forward shake as if he is toasting the crowd with it. The crowd applauds.

Without knowing it, Charlie has just deceived every person in the audience and the millions of people watching on TV and anywhere else the ceremony was being shown. Not because he intentionally wanted to enhance his speech or hide something in his story, or anything of the sort, but because when he said, "… if I remember correctly," he in fact didn't.

Rewind to the day that Charlie referred to in his speech: the day that he credited his introduction to filmmaking and his childhood dream with. The day he was thinking of was Saturday, March 26, 1988. Charlie and Nick were ten years old. They were working on their first short film together using Nick's father's VHS camcorder. Charlie filmed and directed while Nick acted out an adventure through the neighborhood, pretending they were racing against time, trying to rescue a girl who was captured by some indiscriminate villains. They cast Nick's younger sister as the girl and Nick's parents as the villains, improvising lines and scenes with them. Then, Nick and Charlie pieced it all together on the VHS player. They premiered it to Nick's family when they were done. Nick's parents as well as Nick's older brothers told Nick and Charlie how impressive it was. Not just the obligatory compliment that friends and family often give each other, but they were actually impressed. At just ten years old, Nick seemed rather comfortable on camera, and Charlie showed an impressive, natural understanding of cinematic timing, angles, emotion, scene blocking, and so on. The only problem is, it wasn't Charlie. Charlie was home with his parents that Saturday when the film was made. It was Nick's other friend, Steven, who made the film with Nick. Charlie had nothing to do with it.

Four years later, however, when Nick and Charlie were hanging out at Charlie's house the night before starting high school, they were reminiscing about memories together. Throughout elementary and middle school, Charlie and Nick were best friends and hung out with each other the most out of everyone they knew. This caused Nick to simply mix up Charlie with Steven when recalling his memory of making the film. When this mixed-up memory floated to the surface of Nick's consciousness, he blurted it out. "Hey, you remember when we made that short film together?" Nick asked Charlie.

Charlie didn't remember at first but considered that he had likely just forgotten about it. It sounded possible enough. He paused for a moment and then said, "Uh, I think so. I'm not sure if I remember. When was it?"

"Seriously?" Nick exclaimed, surprised that Charlie forgot. "It was like four or five years ago. Sixth grade, maybe. It was with my sister and we had a whole plot to it. It was stupid but kind of cool," Nick said. He reminded Charlie how good he was at filming and directing it, and how impressed his parents and siblings were with it. He told Charlie that he remembered him being a natural at the whole thing.

This made Charlie want the memory to be real, and he began to convince himself that it likely was and he had in fact just forgotten about it. Nick seemed so sure about it, and Charlie trusted Nick. "Oh, yeah! I remember it now," Charlie exclaimed back to Nick. He was still a little unsure when he said this but was starting to find a clearer memory forming in his head, which was enough for Charlie to believe that it was real. In this moment, an entirely false memory was planted in Charlie's brain.

Charlie was experiencing something fairly common. This occurrence happens every day to any number of people. A memory is formed, fabricated, or edited in addition to or in place of what really happened. In psychology, it is known as a confabulation or false memory, understood to be caused by psychological occurrences known as memory conformity, suggestibility, source misattribution, or the misinformation effect, as well as other things. Generally, in all these cases, something like a social influence, individual desire, misjudgment, emotional circumstance, etc., creates an error in the memory retrieval process, and as a result, a memory can end up becoming modified or a false memory can be planted in the brain's memory center.

In 1995, a study found that when a researcher instructed a group of individuals to recall and describe specific childhood memories that were given to the conductor by the participant's parents, if three out of the four memories were real, but one was fake and intentionally suggested to the participant as real, about 25 percent of the participants believed that it was a real memory and went on to describe it vividly and emotionally.

In the first study, the suggested memory was that the participant had gotten lost in a shopping mall as a child and was rescued by an elderly lady. This study was then followed by many other similar studies, which suggested more unusual memories, like almost drowning, being attacked by vicious animals, witnessing satanic possessions, and so on. In all cases, a statistically significant number between 33 percent and 50 percent of all participants agreed that they had experienced the suggested memory and recalled it as real, even though it wasn't. Furthermore, the false memory implantation is found to occur most easily when participants are given information from trustworthy individuals. Nick, being Charlie's best friend, made Charlie naturally susceptible. Generally, a situation like this is benign and doesn't change much, if anything at all. Most memories in general don't. Some, however, change everything.

As Charlie and Nick began high school, the seed of Charlie's false memory started to sprout, causing him to become increasingly interested in film production. Charlie took film classes available at his school, participated in the school's TV station and film club, volunteered at the town's local TV network, and created film projects with Nick. Because of Charlie's false memory, he believed he was already naturally good at filming and directing and editing, which gave him the confidence to take on lead roles in projects, face tough challenges, and take interesting creative risks. As his skills developed and quickly compounded as a result of all this, Charlie became more and more comfortable in high-pressure roles, never doubting his intuition. As more time passed, he began working as a freelance filmmaker with local companies and clients who were looking for video advertising, video tutorials, event coverage, and whatever else.

Charlie was really good. He was the most talented member in the school's film club, his short films were impressive (all things considered), and his clients were more than satisfied with his work. The false memory seemed to be lining up with Charlie's actual abilities.

In college, Charlie and Nick studied film at the same school, collaborating on several film projects that Charlie would write and direct, while Nick would help write and act in. Two of the films won multiple awards at various film festivals. As a profession, Charlie also began to shoot and direct music videos for friends of friends, moving with confidence through each project, never doubting his abilities.

One music video Charlie made was with an artist who was becoming successful and popular in the mainstream simultaneous to working with Charlie. Because of this timing and Charlie's unique, bold approach with the video, the video took off in the music world, and he began working with other major music artists soon after, facilitating the start of his professional career.

As he grew through the music video world, Charlie wrote screenplays and pitches for feature films, determined to accomplish his childhood dream of being a feature film director.

Several years later, in 2004, Charlie's feature film directorial debut was released as an independent film entitled *Delusions of Grandeur*, staring Nick as the lead. That year, it won an Independent Spirit Award for best original screenplay, and with this, Charlie put his stake in Hollywood.

Now, fifteen years later, here Charlie is coming back down from the Dolby Theater stage, holding an Oscar for best director, one of the highest public achievements in all of film.

On the drive home after the award ceremony, Charlie, his wife, his parents, Nick, and a few other friends talk about how surreal the night was. Charlie's wife looks at him and Nick and says, "This is unbelievable. Did you guys ever think you would be leaving the Dolby Theater in a limo with an Oscar?" Charlie smiles at her and then looks at Nick for a moment before answering. Then he says, "Well,

I can't say I ever knew for sure, but I think you're only as capable as you believe you are. Some people aren't nearly as capable as they believe they are. Some people are far more. And some people are exactly right. And you can only find out which one you are by following it to the end. And I guess I'm one of the lucky ones who was right." The small group in the limo marvels at the profound sounding answer, unaware of the incredible and beautiful irony.

The entire basis of Charlie's success was founded on a false memory. Something that he was wrong about. Fortunately for Charlie, he was right about the fact that you are often only as capable as you believe you are, and better yet, perhaps sometimes you only become capable because you believe you are.

Every Person Is One Choice Away from Everything Changing

Carl sat on his couch, looking back and forth between his phone and the ceiling, trying to figure out whether he was about to move ten thousand miles away to Australia, leaving his home, girlfriend, family, friends, job, and whole life behind or not.

The opportunity to move had suddenly come up when his best friend, Novak, decided he would be moving to Australia with his girlfriend. At age twenty-seven, Novak was facing a sort of quarter-life crisis and wanted to try and start something new and venture out into the world while he still felt new himself. Moving to Australia had been both Novak and Carl's dream ever since they were children and their families went there to vacation. They both felt a weird natural connection with the colors, architecture, people, and feeling of the country. They visited again several times throughout their teens and early twenties. On one of their trips, when they were fifteen, Carl and Novak agreed that they would move there when they were older and start a business together. This would remain their dream ever since.

As they grew older, though, like most dreams, it began to take a back seat to reality. Carl went to college for accounting in his hometown of Boston and got a job through a professor right after school, which he couldn't turn down. Novak had a family member who worked for a tech startup in Boston, and as a result, he was given an opportunity to work for the company. However, after four years of Novak working for the company, it was suddenly acquired, and he was out of a job. As part of the layoff, however, he was provided with a nice-sized severance package. And now, with some new extra money and nothing else stopping him, he decided he wanted to start a business and take a major leap of faith in his life. His girlfriend, somewhat of a free spirit, was on board with him.

Novak came up with the idea of moving to Australia and creating an eco-friendly agritech company that utilized Australia's farming industry and demand for local, farm-fresh, organic food.

One month later, Novak told Carl that he and his girlfriend were moving to Australia within the next couple of months. He told him about the business idea that he and his girlfriend worked on together and showed him the beta website and app he created. It looked and sounded great and well thought out. Novak's girlfriend had experience working in logistics, and Novak understood the business and technology side. They were the perfect duo.

When Carl didn't fully understand, Novak explained, "I want you to be a partner in the business, man. You and me move to Australia and live the dream for real! You can run sales, marketing, outreach, budgeting, and all the finances. It'll be perfect!"

With mostly body language, Carl agreed with Novak's enthusiasm.

"Think about how much harder it will get if we don't do this now. Do you really want to stay here forever?" Novak continued, "This business has a real chance to help people. We can help provide families with food who can't afford it and help the planet by contributing to a more sustainable food industry. And we can finally take a real shot at our dream."

After asking a few questions and trying to process everything, Carl replied, "Alright, I need at least a couple days to think about it."

Novak agreed and told him to let him know once he'd thought about it more.

Over the next day, Carl thought about all the factors associated with the decision. He thought about how his mother had passed away just two years ago, and he and his father had become extremely close ever since. His father was not taking it well, and Carl's older brother had a strained relationship with his father. In a way, Carl was all his father had left. He worried that if he left, it would break his father. Carl also thought about his girlfriend, Stephanie. They had only been dating a little more than a year, but he had already started imagining a future with her. Things were going well, and they just seemed to click. He knew that he couldn't expect her to go with him, and he knew a long-distance relationship was bound to fail, if she even agreed to it. He thought about all his other friends and family. He knew it wasn't as if they would cease to exist, but he also knew that in a way, their existence would fade a little. Perhaps for some of them, they would fade so much that it would almost be as if they no longer existed at all.

Then he thought about his current job. He worked for a great firm with great benefits, and he had finally started making some headway in the company. There was a lot of financial promise ahead, and he knew it was the more prudent career bet. But then, at the same time, he thought about how a greater risk meant a potentially greater reward. He didn't mind his current job, but it was fairly tedious and unexciting. He had just happened into it as a means of a conservative career path. He had always dreamed of being a part of building a business and creating a more meaningful impact and legacy for himself. Furthermore, he never particularly liked Boston. He had always wanted to move to the countryside ever since he was a kid. Specifically, he always envisioned a future where he lived in Australia; it was just one of those things that he had convinced himself. And now, at twenty-seven, Carl felt an urge to leave home and forge his own life for himself while he was still young. He wondered how he could turn down such an opportunity to move to his dream location with his best friend and try to build something potentially important and helpful. How could he turn his back on his own vision of his future when it was right in front of him?

For the following three days, Carl thought about the decision every waking second, ruminating back and forth between the potential outcomes of both choices. After four days, it seemed as if no matter how hard he tried, he made no progress in the decision. He remained as unsure of what he should do on the fourth day as the first. It wasn't an equation with numeric values and obvious reasoning. Each option was completely different, with their own entirely different set of variables and values, with no ability to know what any of it equaled.

Carl had purposefully held off sharing the situation with anyone in order to avoid getting anyone upset before he had a better sense of what he was going to do, but by this point, he needed someone else's opinion.

Over the next two days, Carl told his father, his girlfriend, two of his other close friends, and his aunt. He asked each of them what they thought he should do. Everyone gave him different answers. His dad and one of his friends said he should go. His aunt and other friend said he should stay. His girlfriend didn't give him a straight answer, but her tears said everything Carl needed to know. They all had perfectly good, rational explanations for what they suggested. And yet, Carl was no better off. He wondered how each answer could sound equally reasonable but be completely contradictory.

On the sixth night of indecision, Carl went on a walk around the city to try to clear his head. He walked late into the night, all around the city and along the harbor. Eventually, he found himself on a bench facing the water, completely secluded in a sectioned-off corner of a pathway. He sat and thought about how his entire future hinged on this one decision contained inside his head. In his brain was the power to facilitate one move that would shape his entire world forever. And yet, he couldn't even know what choice was right. He thought about how insane this was, to be given the ability to make decisions but not given the ability to ever know the consequences of them. He felt like he was blind and being forced to drive a car. He wished he could just know how both options would play out. Then he would know which one to choose. Overwhelmed, Carl looked out at the stars and moon shimmering against the water. He closed his eyes and took a deep breath.

Suddenly, an old man walked past Carl and sat on a bench just a couple of feet away. This jolted Carl to attention. He was immediately surprised by anyone being in the same secluded pathway and was curious as to why a man who looked to be at least in his eighties would be out alone at 2 a.m. Worried that the man was perhaps unwell or lost, Carl decided to ask him if he was okay. Politely, he turned and leaned over to the man and said, "How's everything going tonight?"

The man slowly turned toward Carl and said, "Good. How 'bout yourself?"

"Good. Is everything okay?" Carl responded.

"Yeah, everything's great. It's a beautiful night, isn't it?"

Carl looked up to the sky. "Yeah. It is." Then they sat quietly.

As Carl jumped back and forth between contemplating his decision again and being distracted by the man's strange presence, the idea of asking the man his opinion occurred to him. He looked over to the man and said, "Can I ask you a question?"

"Sure. Shoot," the man replied.

Carl then went on and described his predicament. He explained the business, his job, his girlfriend, his best friend, his father, and everything else. Then he asked the man what he would do.

The man laughed a little as if he had some experience or insight about the subject that was comical to him. "So, you want to make the right choice, but you don't know what the right choice is?" the old man asked.

"Yeah, exactly. I'm completely lost. I wish I could just know what both would be like, you know?" Carl replied.

"If only," the old man said with another chuckle. "Wouldn't that make everything easier?" They sat quietly for a moment, and then the man said, "What if you just decide right now based on what I choose for you? Someone who basically doesn't know you at all. It'll be like flipping a coin, but the coin has a brain and understands the situation a little."

Somehow this made sense to Carl, and after thinking for a moment, he agreed. He just needed it to be over. The old man paused and then quickly said, "All right, you're going."

Desperately clinging to reason, Carl asked the old man, "What made you choose that?"

"I guess you'll have to find that out," replied the old man.

Carl sat for a moment, processing the fact that he was going to do what the man just said.

When he got up and went to thank the man and wish him a good night, he was gone. Carl figured he must have just left while he was thinking and didn't hear him say goodbye.

Five weeks later, Carl was on a plane with Novak and Novak's girlfriend, headed to Australia.

Twenty years would go by. Carl had remained in Australia ever since he moved. He now considered it home. Even after twenty years, it still felt amazing to him. A walk along the coast or into the countryside never ceased to amaze him and bring him a little peace. He and Stephanie broke up within the first three months of trying to maintain some form of a long-distance relationship. One and a half years later, he met a woman named Natalie and fell in love almost instantly. They got married three years later, and eventually had two healthy boys, who provided Carl with a great source of purpose and love.

Carl, Novak, and Novak's girlfriend's business ran for about six years until unforeseen industry changes, operational problems, and regulations forced them to shut it down. They had tried pivoting the business model several times before it ultimately failed. During this time, however, Carl discovered a surprisingly strong passion for the farming process himself.

A year after the original business ended, Carl bought a small indoor farm facility and started his own personal farming business. The business became profitable in the first three years, but the profit ceiling was low, and it brought in fairly little money each month. His wife, who worked as a freelance copywriter, didn't bring in much money either. Because of the low income and the expenses of two children, the financial burden made Carl and Natalie horrible and bitter to one another. Their personalities just never quite clicked after the early phases of the marriage. They continued to stay together for the kids, but they were miserable.

Carl and Novak remained close during and after the business and formed a nice little friend group with others they met along the way. Even though the original plan didn't work out, Carl felt connected with his work, and contributing directly to a local, sustainable food industry gave him the occasional sense of pride. However, it came at the cost of constant financial burden, heavy stress, and minimal free time. Carl wasn't happy, but he wasn't unhappy. He was a mix of both, depending on the time or day.

As the years went by, Carl visited home less and less. He would go home and visit his father most Christmases and special occasions, but eventually, he started missing a few years here and there.

The last time he visited his father was at his funeral.

At the service, Carl stood looking down at his father's lifeless body. He looked around at old friends, family members, neighbors, his brother, whom he hadn't seen in five years. He looked at his wife. He immediately needed to get some fresh air.

After the service was over, he walked to the bar down the street that he would go to when he was in his twenties. As fate would have it, he passed Stephanie. They noticed each other, hugged, and talked for a little while. Carl told her why he was home, and she said she was sorry. It was weird. He felt at ease, almost as if they didn't miss a beat. He felt more comfortable with her in that moment than he had in a long time. After a little while, they said how great it was to see each other and went their separate ways.

Carl sat at the bar, drinking alone. He thought back to the day he left and felt a weird sense of regret. He wondered if he did the wrong thing leaving his father and family and Stephanie, leaving his good job that would've certainly paid away most of his current problems. He remembered how he let some stranger make such an important decision for him and suddenly felt like his regret wasn't even his, which made him feel exponentially worse.

Later that night, Carl walked around the city by himself to try to clear his head. He walked down the edge of the city, along the harbor. He sat down on the same bench he'd sat on many years ago, facing the water. He sat back in the bench, looking up at the stars, closed his eyes, and breathed in deeply. Suddenly, an old man poked Carl's shoulder. Carl, disoriented, opened his eyes to an old man standing above him. Before Carl could say anything, the old man asked if he was okay. Carl, having realized he must have passed out on the bench, told the man he was fine and just fell asleep. The old man sat on the bench a few feet away as he explained to Carl how it was unsafe to fall asleep alone in such an area. "You're likely to get robbed or something," he said.

Carl agreed and said it was an accident. He explained to the old man that he hadn't been able to get much sleep the last several days because he had been trying to make a decision about whether or not he would be moving to Australia.

After talking for a little while and explaining his predicament about the business, his best friend, his girlfriend, his father, and everything else, Carl had the idea to ask the old man what he thought he should do. The man laughed a little as if he had some experience or insight about the subject that was comical to him. After a little more conversation, the man said, "What if you just decide right now based on what I choose? Someone who basically doesn't know you at all. It'll be like flipping a coin, but the coin has a brain and understands the situation a little." Stricken with a weird sense of déjà vu, Carl agreed. He just needed it to be over. The old man paused for a moment and then quickly said, "All right, you're staying."

Desperately clinging to reason, Carl asked, "Why? What made you choose that?"

"I guess you'll have to find that out," said the old man.

Five weeks later, Novak was on a plane for Australia, while Carl ate dinner with Stephanie and his father.

Twenty years would go by. Carl had stayed in the Boston area ever since. He climbed the ranks in his career field and became chief financial officer for a nice, midsize company. He was now making an incredible salary. He married Stephanie a couple years after deciding to stay. They decided against having children because Stephanie was against it, and Carl wasn't sure himself and was willing to concede. Over the years, their love grew stronger and stronger. They fought like any couple, but there was a luster to their relationship that's rare and always present. They seemed to just click, as if their personalities were meant to work together. Their relationship provided Carl with a great source of love and purpose in life.

Carl had also remained close with his father and helped him into his old age. They maintained a close bond that Carl cherished. Most of Carl's other friends, however, had moved away or drifted apart. Novak and Carl sort of lost contact as well, only seeing each other once every year or so, if that. With no children and a higher income, money had never really been an issue, and his personal life became fairly stress free. He never really came around to liking his job, though. As he climbed the corporate ranks, it came with increasing bureaucratic tedium, and he felt a sense of pointlessness and absurdity in it all. The longer he stayed, though, the harder it was to leave. As he aged, he found a sense of boredom, hollowness, and social isolation in his life. He wasn't happy, but he wasn't unhappy. He was a mix of both, depending on the time or day.

On his forty-eighth birthday, Carl had a party. Novak flew out, along with a couple of other old friends. At the party, Carl spent a good deal of time catching up with Novak, and Novak told him all about the last couple of years in Australia. He told him how his three kids were doing and how well the business was doing. Carl asked Novak about some details in the business, and Novak explained how their third partner, whom they had found when they first moved and who had helped them get the business through some hard times, was now playing a key role in the business moving into foreign markets. He told Carl that the business was helping thousands of families each month, and he was extremely proud of it. Then he told Carl he wished he would have been the person he was talking about instead. Carl saw the pride and enthusiasm in Novak's eyes when he spoke about his children and his business. Carl looked around at his coworkers, at his apartment. He suddenly felt a sense of doubt and regret in his life's path. He wondered if he did the wrong thing. He thought about how he had let some stranger make such an important choice for him. The worst part wasn't even that his life was bad or good, but that in this moment, it almost felt like it wasn't even his to regret.

At the end of the night, after almost everyone had gone home, Carl went on a walk around the city by himself, moderately drunk. He walked down the edge of the city, along the harbor. He sat down on the same bench he sat on many years ago, facing the water. He sat back in the bench, looked up at the stars, closed his eyes, and breathed in deeply. Suddenly, someone poked Carl on the shoulder. Carl, disoriented, opened his eyes to an old man standing above him. Before Carl could say anything, the old man asked if he was okay.

Carl, having realized he must have passed out, told the man he was okay and just fell asleep. The old man sat on the bench a few feet away as he explained to Carl how it was unsafe to fall asleep alone in such an area. "You're likely to get robbed or something," he said. Carl agreed and said it was an accident. He explained to the old man that he hadn't been able to get much sleep the last several days because he had been trying to decide whether or not he was going to move to Australia. Carl explained the situation with the business, his best friend, his girlfriend, his father, and everything else. As he did, Carl felt a weird sense of clarity. He couldn't put his finger on it, but he almost felt like he knew what each decision would be like, like he had already lived them. But despite this, he still had no clue which one was right.

The old man interrupted. "What if you just decide right now based on what I choose? Someone who basically doesn't know you at all. It'll be like flipping a coin, but the coin has a brain and understands the situation a little."

Carl thought for a moment and then politely said, "No. I think I need to decide myself. Thank you, though."

"I thought you said you couldn't figure out which choice was right," said the old man. "How are you going to get past that?"

"I guess ... I'm not," replied Carl. "I spent the last week trying to figure out which choice was right, but maybe there isn't a right choice. Maybe there's just a choice."

"What do you mean by that?" interrupted the old man.

"Maybe some decisions aren't hard because there's a better option but because there isn't one. This whole time I've been worried about regretting my choice by choosing the wrong thing, as if I could even know what I'm regretting. Regret would mean there was a right choice, and I made the wrong one. But how could there be a wrong one? The only thing I can know is that on the other side of the decision, I'll be there. And if I'm there, no matter what path I go, there'll always be something to love, and there'll always be something to dread. And the only thing to regret would be not making the decision for myself. If you pick it, if anyone else picks it, if I leave it up to chance, it'll never be mine. Or at least it won't feel like it."

"So, how do you choose now?"

"I guess I do my best, pick one, and move on," replied Carl. "It won't be chance. It won't be certainty. It'll be somewhere in between. And that'll be the right choice."

"So," said the old man with a continued smile, "which are you going to choose?"

Hidden Universes

A microorganism happens into favorable enough conditions to duplicate its DNA and multiply. In an instant, an entirely new microorganism is rendered into existence.

This new microbe looks out at an array of colors and objects. Confused, it turns to its parent microbe and asks, "What am I?"

"Alive," the parent microbe says matter-of-factly and then swims off, leaving the new microbe to itself.

The new microbe is hungry and confused. It swims out across the vast landscape of its surroundings, pulled by things it doesn't understand; instructions written into its DNA, passed down from a lineage of three billion years of prior parent microbes.

Compelled by its genetic code, the new microbe begins eating and adapting to its circumstances, graduating through the ranks of its community, and engaging in a system of trillions and trillions of other microbes. Every day, it works, eats, and communicates with other members of the system it's associated with, making changes in itself and trying to maintain order in its surroundings.

As the microbe ages, though, it becomes increasingly curious of what it is and what it's doing. It was only ever told that it was alive, after all, and then it just started doing things. It wonders what *alive* even means. And why so little an explanation? It questions why it just goes around all day, working to survive and surviving to work. *For what?* it wonders. *What's the point of it all?*

The weight of these thoughts increasingly bears down on the microbe's motivation, but something in it, or out of it, keeps it going. It struggles through a period of apathy, but it soon becomes somewhat fueled by its desire to resolve these thoughts, counterbalancing the negative effects of its confusion with intrigue and curiosity. It's almost as if the microbe basically has no choice in the matter: whether it cares to know what it is or isn't and how this affects it. In all cases, its desire to keep living and carry out its role seems to just endure inside the microbe all the same.

The microbe continues on, working and fulfilling its role, while spending much of its life looking for answers. It talks with other microbes in its community about what they think. It travels to other communities comprising different microbes and asks them. It looks around every corner, under every object, and into every thing. It studies. It learns. It offers itself to all sorts of ideas, never quite finding one that seems to hold. Every time it thinks it's found an answer, the answer eventually collapses in on itself, and the microbe moves on to something else. Trying to find the point of everything becomes the point of everything for the microbe.

Each night, whenever it has the chance, the microbe looks up at the seemingly unending darkness above it sprinkled with particles and various formations. It looks at the motion of everything that surrounds it: the bodies of liquid infinitely pushing and pulling all on their own, the air breathing back and forth, the branches of something extending upward and swaying about. The microbe considers all the ideas and explanations it has heard and learned, all the theories it has synthesized on its own. It wonders, on and on, what it all must be.

Because of its limited perception, however, it never has nor ever will come anywhere close to guessing that it is a gut bacterium inside the intestines of a human body named Ariel. Ariel, an incomprehensibly larger organism, is entirely dependent on this microbe, as well as most of the trillions of others inside and on her. She is, however, mostly unaware of this entire microbial universe that she houses.

This one particular microbe, known as a *bacteroides fragilis*, is essential to Ariel's food digestion. She and the microbe persist in a feedback-loop relationship, Ariel providing the microbe with its environment, food, and life, and the microbe helping Ariel stay alive, assisting her health and mood regulations by digesting fibers, providing her nutrients, and communicating with her brain. Essentially, without knowing it, every time the microbe was unhealthy, disengaged, or sedentary, Ariel suffered, and vice versa. Furthermore, if either Ariel or the microbes gave up and stopped entirely, the other could die, ending their entire particular *universe*.

In this moment, Ariel is sitting at the end of a pier at a beach. It's late in the evening on a Thursday. She has had a long day at work. She's been struggling to find motivation, but something in her, or out of her, keeps her going. It's almost as if she basically has no choice in the matter.

She eats some takeout as she looks up at the seemingly unending darkness of the night sky sprinkled with particles and various formations. She looks at the motion of everything that surrounds her: the ocean infinitely pushing and pulling all on its own, the air ceaselessly breathing back and forth, the branches of the trees swaying about. She looks out and wonders what it all is. What it all must be for.

Because of her limited perception, though, she'll never come anywhere close to knowing what she is inside of nor how important she is to it.

Getting Stuck in Déjà Vu

It started when I was young. I would feel a weird sense that I had already experienced what I was experiencing. I would go somewhere or see something for the first time and recognize it like I had been there or seen it before. The first time it happened, it scared me so badly, I cried to my mother and asked her why everything felt so weird. She told me that it was normal, that it was a thing called déjà vu, and I didn't need to worry about it. At that age, I basically believed anything my parents said, and even though it still scared me, I trusted her.

Of course, when my mom told me it was déjà vu, she didn't actually know what it was or why it was "normal." No one did. Déjà vu was a phenomenon of the brain that science didn't really understand. And beyond that, no one else could have ever been in my head to really understand or know what I was truly experiencing.

As I grew into my teenage years, it became even more intense and increasingly difficult to ignore. A trigger, be it a visual image or an odor or a thought or an emotion or everything all at once, would seem to cause the gears of everything to stop turning, and it would feel as though time stopped and I became stuck in a moment. Whenever this happened, it almost seemed as if I could see things around me in time the same way I could see things around me in physical space. It was as if to my left was the past and to my right was the future, and the present was exactly and only where my body was. I tried to just rationalize it away, convincing myself it was just some strange, normal thing, but when I explained it to my friends and family, they didn't really understand. They said that they all had their own unusual experiences of déjà vu, but none of them shared what I described. This kind of scared me, but it quickly became one of those things that was easier to deal with by not dealing with it, so I didn't.

Then, when I was around nineteen or twenty, I was sitting at the kitchen table in my parents' house. I was eating soup and watching TV when a déjà vu hit me, a sense that I had already watched the episode of the show I was watching, which I certainly had not, paired with a sense that my brother and father were about to walk into the house from the side door. Then, in the next moment, they did. I told my brother and father what happened as they settled into the kitchen. We agreed it was just a strange coincidence and laughed it off together. It terrified me, though, and I couldn't sleep the next couple of nights.

Then it kept happening. I would have the sense that I already experienced what I was about to experience, and sometimes it would seem to come true. Along with myself, my parents and friends became incapable of ignoring it. My parents were rather disturbed by it, and we decided it was time to talk to a doctor.

To the best of my abilities, I explained to my doctor what was happening. She essentially had no clue what was going on beyond just general theories of déjà vu, which were, of course, inconclusive and of no help. She found my situation to be exceptionally abnormal. Déjà vu was common, she said, but the intensity and frequency of my experiences were concerningly unusual, by her understanding. She decided it would be best if I saw a neurologist.

After a period of tests, evaluations, brain scans, and so on, the neurologist found nothing wrong with my brain, and also struggled to diagnose me beyond just an unusual case of déjà vu. However, he

THE HIDDEN STORY OF EVERY PERSON

predicted that I might have some temporal lobe damage and was experiencing seizures during the episodes. He referred me to an epileptologist, a doctor specializing in epileptic seizures.

I explained to the epileptologist what I explained to everyone—that when it came on, it felt like my relationship with time didn't exist. Not that time didn't exist at all, but more like time and I broke up for a few moments. I explained that during these moments, it sometimes seemed like I knew what someone was about to say a few seconds before they said it, or what commercial was about to come on TV next, or if someone was going to enter a room, and that sometimes it actually seemed to happen.

After more tests and evaluations, he basically confirmed what the neurologist predicted and surmised that I was having mini-seizures, which were inciting vivid hallucinatory déjà vus and causing me to see and connect things that weren't actually real. He said that the seizures were causing a flurry of neurons to fire all at once throughout my brain, causing my conscious understanding of things and unconscious processing of things to get mixed up and fall out of sync. In other words, I was perceiving things that weren't happening in the way or order that they were actually happening. The sense that something had already happened or was going to happen was a result of my perceptual experience occurring earlier or later than my conscious comprehension. This made a lot of sense and was a huge relief.

However, the epileptologist went on and said that there was nothing showing any evidence of damage or alteration in my brain on the EEG, CT, or MRI brain scans, but said that this didn't rule out the diagnosis, and that normal brain scan readings didn't necessarily mean I had a normal brain, and that the problem was likely just not physically manifesting itself. I wanted more than anything to believe him, but I got the sense that, even though he was an expert, he wasn't really sure. And when I asked how that would explain the fact that when I would tell someone else that something was about to happen and they would confirm my prediction when it did, he didn't really have an answer and just brushed it off as a coincidence or a part of the whole mental disorientation of the seizure. I hoped he was right but struggled to fully believe he was. And despite how similar they might seem, hoping and believing are two completely different things.

In response to the diagnosis, the epileptologist prescribed me Dilantin, an anti-epileptic medication, as well Lexapro, an anti-anxiety medication. The epilepsy medication didn't stop the episodes from occurring, and the anxiety medication made me nauseous and numb. After about a month of waiting and hoping the anti-epileptic medication would begin to work, it never did. The doctor began to discuss some alternative methods and the possibility of some procedures that might help. However, the problem was we had to determine exactly what and where something was wrong in my brain before we could procedurally correct it.

While I continued tests and evaluations, the déjà vu episodes continued. They seemed to get even more intense and weren't merely brief, momentary sensations anymore, but prolonged episodes in which I became nearly incapacitated.

Then, one day while I was at work, everything broke. It was as if something had been building up inside me, and once it became sufficiently heavy enough, it cracked the surface of everything. It felt like I could see behind the curtains of reality and saw all the things that went into creating the show but would never otherwise see as a part of the audience. I saw the choreography of all the particles dancing in and out of nothing. I heard the music of all the quarks and electrons vibrating in the background of every object. I saw the mask of time and the set design of space. I saw the reason for the chaos and the meaning of the meaninglessness. I saw the spotlight of existence isolated on one small spot, center stage, and the darkness of oblivion just one small step behind it. Then I saw my whole life all at once, like if each frame of a movie were laid out on a table and you could see the first and last scene with a slight adjustment of the eyes. And just like how a series of movie frames is only experienced as a movie in time by playing it through a projector or DVD player or file player, I saw that I was the projector, DVD player, and file player of my life. And that the whole thing was all already there, just like how a full movie is always on the film reel, DVD, or file, no matter what part of it you are watching.

It was a strange, ineffable flurry of what I can only describe as rapidly fast-forwarding and rewinding everything in my life. And just like watching a movie fast-forwarded or rewound at six-times speed, it was blurry and hard to process, but I could catch the main ides of scenes as my unconscious mind worked to fill in the blanks. Then, suddenly, I found myself at the end. And at the end, I saw the end of everything. Not merely the end of my life, but the end of everyone's. I saw the Earth moving toward the sun. Or the sun toward the Earth. I saw the world burning as it degraded into chaos. I saw that all of humanity was, during my lifetime, going to die in a catastrophe of some random cosmic circumstance. Then, as if the director of the show realized its mistake, the curtains pulled back to their proper place, and I came to, into the most overwhelming state of panic, disorientation, and paranoia.

It took me about a week to even begin to recover, and frankly, I never fully recovered at all. I worked so hard to rationalize the experience; to convince myself it was a dream, or a psychotic episode, or literally anything else. After I finally built up enough stamina, I told my parents and girlfriend and doctor about it.

I went through another round of brain scans and tests, and still, nothing wrong was found. The doctor essentially concluded the same original diagnosis, and he and my parents worked to convince me that it was just a severe epileptic episode and was not real in the way that I felt it to be. I was incapable of fully coming to terms with this. I wasn't sure what happened or what was real, but I struggled to ignore the possibility of what it was or could've been. It's hard to see or feel something and be convinced by someone else that you didn't, just because they didn't. How could anyone else know what I experienced inside my head without having been there themselves? And how could anyone else actually know whether or not I was experiencing something real? Even if it was an epileptic episode, I wondered if that was actually more real than my normal sense of real. What if everything that was real, day-to-day, was only real according to the conditions of my normal mind, but during these moments of all my brain neurons firing at once, I experienced what was actually real—the conditions of reality outside of myself, without all the filters and lenses and perceptual parameters my brain worked to hold up in every other moment? I tried talking this through with my parents and girlfriend, and then the next time I saw my doctor, he increased my medication, referred me to a psychologist, and began to seriously consider the implementation of an electronic brain stimulator to counter abnormal brain activity.

I spent some amount of the following year or so trying to talk with officials and scientists and cosmologists and whoever else might be able to look into the possibility of issues with the sun or celestial patterns or any other potential signs of problems. No one took me seriously. I seemed crazy, and I knew it. I gave up and receded into isolation.

The biggest problem was that in the moments of the déjà vus or premonitions or whatever it was, even if it seemed like I could tell that something was going to happen, I often wouldn't know exactly when or if I was right until after, especially for farther away events. There were no dates or certainties in the world of déjà vus and premonitions. And so, I lived in fear, not only about whether my premonition of the world's end was true, but when it might occur, if it did.

As I got older, I continued to experience intense déjà vu, premonitory breaches of everything like that first one. They were all essentially the same. And despite their continuation, nothing physically wrong was ever found with my brain. Far worse and more terrifying, some of the senses and visuals I had during them began to come true, and my life appeared to in fact be relatively synced up with whatever it was. I began to realize more and more that it was likely something beyond seizures. In this, I began to feel the imminence of the end of the world, as if it was already there; an inescapable cycle between sadness for what would soon be lost and an anxiety about when.

My relationship with my girlfriend fell apart as I found myself struggling to love her with the knowledge that I would lose her with the rest of the world. Knowing that everything was going to end made everything slippery and transient, impossible to commit to or

THE HIDDEN STORY OF EVERY PERSON

care about. I stopped caring about my job and my goals and my aspirations. I couldn't find motivation to do much of anything, knowing that whatever I did, whoever I cared about, and whatever I became interested in, I would lose. The dysphoria between me and the rest of the world further isolated and saddened me. Everyone was going about everything as normal, chasing moments and things, attaching to stuff, committing to stuff, trying to solve stuff, taking everything so seriously. But no one knew or cared to know that it was all about to end forever.

I exerted whatever efforts I had toward trying to master the déjà vu and premonition experience. Now that I found myself recurringly sensing what was going to happen in the future, I found myself desperate to try to do something about it. I thought that if I could slow down or control the déjà vu/premonition experience, I could find a solution to the impending end of everything and escape it. Nothing worked.

Then, many years later, it began to happen. A massive rogue planet floated into our solar system, destabilized Earth's orbit, and pushed us toward the sun. I was right. Or whatever the premonition was, was right.

As scientists began to understand what was happening, experts predicted about two to three months before a collision with the sun, if we didn't collide with Venus or Mercury first. The Earth had about two to three weeks before everything was so hot, the surface would melt. This was initially faced with worldwide denial and skepticism. Then, as the size of the sun began to increase, the world slowly began to realize. The doom of the entire species and its entire heritage of species. The closing chapter. The final scene, with no credits. This realization was followed by mass hysteria and chaos. The leaders of the world broke down. Mass suicides. Pillaging. And far, far worse.

When this happened, and my final premonition came true, I was eighty-seven years old. Just nine years under the life expectancy of my generation. I essentially had lived a full life, at least in terms of years.

In the approaching final moments, as the light increased and the darkness approached, I sat alone in a chair on my porch and watched the sun grow. I drank whiskey as I reflected on how unfathomably real, yet science-fiction the situation was. In this moment, I realized that the whole time, I knew that the world was going to end, and I had a choice that came with that awareness. I had the choice to live in spite of my foresight or live in fear of it. And I chose the wrong one. How foolish was I to know that the world would soon end, and I didn't spend every possible moment enraptured by it and in complete delight over the fact that it had not yet? I essentially wasted my whole life worrying about whether I would live a full life, which caused me to live a very shallow one. The true catastrophe wasn't the end of the world, but how I lived before it ended. I was, in the most ironic way possible, sad about losing the world and not being alive, while I was alive and the world was still there. Like never wearing your favorite pair of shoes because you're afraid you're going to get them dirty, I ruined the thing that I feared losing with the fear of losing it. And then, just like I knew I would the whole time, I lost it.

One Thought Can Change You Forever

C asey had had this type of experience before but never quite like this. It wasn't a panic attack, per se, but certainly somewhere in the same vein of experience. A moment when everything he understood and felt to be true started to crack and peel back, the world shedding its skin and revealing an entirely new image of itself to him.

Casey had just finished watching another video on the topic of free will, or more specifically, the lack thereof. Up until more recently, Casey never really paid much interest to this or any similar topic. That kind of stuff always seemed distant, abstract, and unnecessary to him. Of course he had free will. He felt it in every moment. What could possibly be the issue or question? But more recently, as he had become slightly older and more curious, he found it a bit harder to see things so simply and find meaning so easily. Consequently, he had become more interested in topics of philosophy, looking further into different ideas in attempts of better self-understanding and ways of living. And now, after having finished this last video, Casey began to question the obviousness of his own free will.

Specifically, the video was about the concept of determinism, which argues that all events, including human action and thought, are determined exclusively by prior causes. It argues for this by claiming that since all particles and phenomena in the universe operate off of cause-and-effect patterns in which there is a continual chain of preceding explanations, then human action and choice must also be subject to the same deterministic system. Logically, this made complete sense to Casey. He did not choose the parents he was born to, where he was born, the brain or genetics he was born with, or the first thoughts and experiences he had. And yet, these things directly affected and led to every thought and experience he had thereafter in an unbroken, linear sequence of cause and effect: a cascading of forces and circumstances that he was not in control of or totally aware of at any point. And thus, every new spur thereafter—everything that felt like his choosing—was yet another product of some fixed, causal thing that he didn't choose beforehand. As a sort of cliched attempt at a witty example, the video he just watched even said within the video itself how he clicked on the video without choosing as a result of the sequence of events tracking back to and beyond his birth, the advent of the internet, the invention of the computer, the formation of the Earth, all the way back to the beginning of the universe. Fundamentally, Casey agreed with this premise of determinism, but he struggled to see how its implications could possibly be true. He struggled to agree with the idea that he himself did not have the free will that he felt in every moment. And in this, Casey experienced the intense, disorienting dissonance that occurs when a truth that one feels intuitively confronts and contradicts a truth that one knows logically. And his intuition fought back. He wondered to himself what could possibly be the point of life if this were true. The video he just watched seemed to claim that he could still choose to enjoy life and find meaning in it. But how? What sense did this make? How could he choose anything now? How can you reconcile the belief that all of existence is deterministic with the belief that you can find your own meaning in the absurdity? It mustn't be completely true, then, Casey rationalized in his head.

Over the following several days, Casey considered and tried a number of different things in a hopeful effort to prove this to himself: to find a flaw in the argument against free will.

On the Tuesday of that week, on his way home from work, to get some fresh air and relax for a little, Casey stopped at a small park not far from his apartment. He sat on a bench, looking out at all the people moving around the park, ruminating to himself. Eventually, still struggling to shake the topic off the surface of his mind, Casey found himself thinking about the concept of free will again. He considered how, in this moment, he and he alone wanted to stop at the park. There was no specific reason or event that caused him to do so. No biological or physiological necessity. No external force. Nothing other than his own willful desire. He wanted to stop at the park, and so, he chose to. And since he chose to, he did. *How is this not free will?* He wondered to himself.

While he continued to think back and forth, a parkgoer's dog happened to run up to where Casey was sitting, sniffing the ground around him profusely. After circling around Casey a couple of times, the dog went on in the other direction, continuing to sniff and follow its nose. As Casey amusedly observed the dog, he considered to himself if the dog had any free will. Clearly the dog wanted to find what it was smelling, and it was choosing to follow what it wanted, but was it choosing to want what it was smelling? No. It was being pulled by a desire that it had no say in.

Of course, Casey knew that he was at least some good amount more conscious than the dog, but did this fundamentally allow him to decide what he did or didn't want any more than the dog? He could choose to do what he wanted, but could he choose to want what he wanted? Sure, he chose to go to the park because he wanted to, but why did he want to? He reflected on where this desire came from and couldn't find anything other than a void. It simply emerged into his consciousness from some unknown stream of events, information, thoughts, and desires that he was mostly unaware of and did not control. If he could have wanted to want to go to the park, wouldn't he have also had to have wanted to want to want to? And then he would have had to have wanted to want to want to want to, so on and so forth into infinity, which of course, he did not and could not have done. In truth, he concluded, he was no different than the dog being pulled by its nose, conditioned by the treats it finds along the way. He was sitting at the park under no free will of his own.

Three days later, on Friday night, Casey was out getting dinner and drinks with a few friends. Once they were seated at the restaurant, Casey decided fairly quickly what he wanted to order: honey BBQ chicken wings. While he waited for the rest of the group to decide what they wanted, he ruminated in his head about what was happening around him. At some point, Casey suddenly had the idea to try something: to choose to order something else that he didn't and wouldn't ever actually want to eat. *Surely*, he thought to himself, *since I'd be doing what I don't want for no reason, without being forced to by anyone or anything other than myself, I'd be acting on my own free will and overriding any deterministic sequence.* Logically, in this moment, this made great sense to Casey, and so, when the waiter came, he ordered a completely different fish meal that he had no desire to eat. When he did this, knowing that it was something Casey didn't like, two of his friends reacted with surprise. One asked him if he liked fish now. Casey, trying not to sound too crazy, briefly explained to them why he ordered what he did. Inevitably, he sounded pretty crazy. After briefly discussing the idea together, one of his friends casually said, "But technically, didn't you still do what you wanted?" This simple question shut the whole thing down for Casey. He immediately realized his friend was right.

In truth, he wanted to prove his sense of free will to himself more than he wanted to order a meal that he would've otherwise wanted to eat. This, although convoluted, was just another *want* that he didn't ultimately choose. Why he wanted to prove his free will in this moment more than getting the meal, Casey could not say. It emerged the same way as all other desires: a result of all the information and thoughts and qualities of his temperament leading up to that moment, going all the way back to his birth and beyond. And so, this attempt to escape the cause-and-effect sequence was itself determined by the very same sequence. In trying to escape the system and prove he had free will, Casey only stepped forward right into it, revealing that he did not. The only difference was now he had a meal he didn't want.

On the following Monday, on his way to work, Casey stopped at a local coffee shop. Upon ordering, the barista asked Casey if he wanted cream or sugar in his coffee. For some reason, this question suddenly spurred an insight and idea in Casey's mind. Somewhat awkwardly, he replied, "I ... don't know." And then waited to see what would happen. Naturally, the barista paused and waited in confusion, assuming Casey would follow through and make the decision. Casey did nothing.

After a few extra-long seconds, in order to finally cut the moment, the barista spoke up and said, "Wait, so you don't want them, or you don't know if you want them?"

After another brief pause, Casey replied, "Yeah, you just pick."

"It doesn't really work like that," the barista replied with a somewhat impatient confusion, "You either want cream and sugar or you don't."

Casey, thinking about how foolish this statement sounded to him now, took a coin out of the little tip container on the counter, flipped it into the air, and caught it. He saw that it landed heads on his hand and then clumsily said, "No cream or sugar. Sorry. Thank you." And then he put the coin back into the container.

While waiting for his order, Casey considered how since he had left the decision up to chance, the outcome was totally random, not determined by any cause-and-effect sequence or any internal or external force leading up to the outcome. For the moment, he felt an excited sense that he was perhaps on to something: a breaking of the whole system.

During the rest of his drive to work, Casey drank some of his coffee, wishing he had gotten cream and sugar. It didn't take more than a few sips for him to realize the absurdity of what he just did. He wanted cream and sugar but got black coffee. Where was the free will in that? He had no say in the random outcome of the coin flip, and so, sure it was random, but how could there be any free will in randomness? If anything, he realized this encounter with the barista was only an elaborate example of even less free will, with just some additional awkwardness and no cream or sugar.

As more days passed, Casey found himself incapable of finding any loopholes—any cases where he could conclusively find examples of the free will that he once felt and knew he had. He watched countless videos, read books and essays on the topic, and so on. At this point, he found it nearly impossible to deny. The sense that he was the controlling force of his life, it seemed, was in fact an illusion. And this was no longer some abstract idea. Now, he felt it clearly and totally. The switch clicked, and the world looked different.

The weight of this troublesome truth hit Casey fairly hard as it fell down onto his shoulders. He now found himself in the unfortunate position that afflicts all human beings: he couldn't unknow what he now knew, even if he wanted to. He couldn't go back to ignorance. Ignorance is certainly not a choice. One cannot choose to truly be ignorant of what they already know, for this would require that they didn't know it to begin with. And Casey realized now that he never even really had a choice in knowing what he did or didn't at all.

That night, he experienced what can only be described as one of the hardest existential crises he'd yet experienced in his life. He struggled to see any point anymore—any meaning. This built up so heavily that later the same night, Casey decided to essentially stop caring, stop trying, stop doing anything really. After all, since he was never really doing anything to begin with, what difference would this make? For the rest of the night, he sat on his couch and stared at the wall with no intention of intentionally doing anything else—a renunciation of his life in a radical act of complete fatalism.

After several hours of sitting, around midnight, Casey became kind of hungry. Naturally, after tolerating the hunger for as long as he could, he got up and made himself a grilled cheese sandwich with a little pizza sauce. Then, he returned to the couch and ate it. He enjoyed it thoroughly. At around 12:55 a.m., he felt that he had to use the bathroom, and naturally, after no longer being able to tolerate the feeling, he got up and went. Then, he returned to the couch feeling much better. Eventually, at around 2:45 a.m., Casey became sufficiently tired and dozed off.

Over the next couple days, he continued sitting, trying to do nothing, scrolling through his phone most of the time in between staring at the wall. It took no more than a day and a half to begin to feel the absolute absurdity of what he was doing. Still weighed down by his sense of pointlessness, though, he stayed put, acting as passively as he could. Eventually, the boredom and desire to do something became so bad, he took out a video game, which he couldn't even remember the last time he played—any video game for that matter. He was surprised the console even still worked.

He started playing and quickly fell into the game, starting the story mode from the beginning and enjoying all the various tasks and challenges along the way. Before he even realized how long he had been playing, he finished the game. Granted, he had already played and beaten the same game when he was younger, but nonetheless, it still felt nice. The time seemed to fly right by. As he watched the final scene of the video game's story conclude, in the sort of corny, typical video game tone, one of the characters said, "Everything is mostly sorted out now. Couldn't have done it without you. Not a total happy ending, but good enough."

Between all the time Casey had to think over the last two days and this line in the video game, in this moment, it hit Casey. The missing piece that put the whole thing back together. He realized he had just thoroughly enjoyed a video game that he knew was fake and had already played. All of the challenges in the game were predetermined and precoded, and the game operated with specific borders, rules, and controls that all worked toward a story that essentially had just one single path to one single predetermined end. Casey fundamentally had no control over how the game was played and where it went. He was just following the storyline as it already existed, experiencing the illusion of him actually creating and performing it. And yet, despite this and his knowledge of it, there he had been, totally and fully immersed, enjoying and finding meaning in it the whole way through. And his active participation was entirely necessary to the experience and the game playing through.

Casey realized that there was no other way to live. There was no escaping the illusion if the illusion was him. But there was no need to. Knowing something is an illusion does not stop the illusion from working. Illusions are illusions because they work. *I am not my perceptions*, he thought to himself, *not my choices, not my actions, but I am still the experiencer of the whole, an observer of a consciousness that can observe and navigate and find meaning in the world. The greatest and most beautiful illusion ever created and experienced, and I have a front-row seat to it. Nothing changes. The illusion is real.*

Not long after this moment, one of Casey's friends called him and asked if he wanted to meet him and a few friends at a local bar. Casey said he did, and within the hour, he got ready, left his apartment, met up with his friends, and enjoyed the rest of the night—the same as he always had.

The Man Who Floated Away into Space

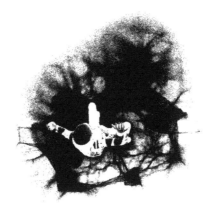

I 'm not sure how long it's been. My only reference points now are distant stars and planets that basically all look the same and don't appear to be moving much from here. The radio and guidance system cut out some time ago, and the manual propulsion system engines were damaged in the initial collision. I've since been drifting alone and disconnected in some unknown direction toward something or nothing. I suppose both are sort of the same to me at this point. I can only assume I'm moving rather fast, considering the speed at which we were hit, but it honestly feels more like I'm just floating in place, like I'm submerged in a literal infinity pool with no edge or surface. My only hope left is that this is some strange dream or hallucination, and I am still on the ground somewhere, soon to come back to reality at any moment.

Admittedly, early on, when the reality of this whole situation first started to set in, I seriously considered that as a possibility. I guess *hoped* might be more accurate—my brain's imaginative, wishful nature trying to conjure up and sustain its last bit of artificial hopefulness, almost convincing me that what is real isn't, and vice versa.

I have since given up such hope. At least of that form. I realized around the same time that I had a decision to make, to either continue on in terror and paranoia fueled by the hope that there was something to be done, something I could do, some other way this whole thing could go; or I could sit back and enjoy the stars. The decision was pretty obvious.

I am going to die. And no one can save me. And I only have so much time left. And I am going to enjoy it.

I float through the void now, free. Perhaps more than I have ever felt or imagined before, totally and completely free.

I feel infinity play with my limbs, as its laws of motion carry me, like a child's plush toy. I just let it. I do not flail. I do not fight it. I just float. I think about where it might be taking me, where I will end up, what distant space I will float on to, what my final view of everything will be.

You know, I have seen this same night sky nearly every night of my life, and I have had the great fortune of being in a profession that has given me the opportunity to see it from all sorts of different angles, close and afar. But right now, swallowed up by it totally, with no sight of home, further out than perhaps anyone has ever been, it looks completely different. Or perhaps it feels completely different. Either way, in this, I realize now more than ever just how used to the insanity of everything we so easily become—to the grave, imminent dangers of living and moving through an unending and unknown space; the unfathomable depth of potential and mystery that is just a short float above our heads at all times. I can't help but laugh to myself at how bored we so easily become, how much we struggle to be dazzled by awe and silenced by humility. We must be the only thing cursed with the tendency to reduce the magnificent to tedium, to analyze beauty into ugliness, to reduce our incredible position to misery.

We are so small. It took no more than one cycle of oxygen for essentially all clear traces of home to disappear from my vision forever. All the greatest heroes and sages and leaders and so on, from here, I don't see any of them.

We forget that we are a life still in its adolescent years, at best, yet to even really leave home. Our species is still filled with the angst and juvenile rebellion of a teenager. The universe must laugh at our arrogant ignorance, our smug righteousness, our poutiness. We still think we know everything, but we know damn near nothing about anything.

Like our pioneering ancestors of every form discovered lands and worlds and ways of being that we take for granted now as the status quo, great unknown lands of the future await us—great unknown manners and knowledge of how to live and be. Unknown turmoil too. Causalities of this kind and far, far worse, of course. To grow up, to age, to toy with the universe and venture out into the unknown always carries its great uncertainty and risk. But it is perhaps one of the most beautiful imperatives of our kind to do so. To live is to be afraid. But perhaps to center that fear on something that unites and grows and reveals wonder is to be afraid with some purpose. I don't know. What else could life possibly be but a series of new horizons, new views; a constant rediscovery of beauty and wonder? I am going to die a casualty of this cause, and I wouldn't want it any other way.

If I have any remaining wish, it's that this was not all in vain: this fatal mission and every pair of shoulders that it stood on, every prior fatal mission, every prior successful mission. I hope that more and more of my kind will see and feel what I do right now, with less finality and more intention. To continue on into the darkness, bringing the lights of their own creation, illuminating the heavens and revealing them as new homes.

Today, the great frontiers are above us. Into the once-believed heavens that we need not be dead to touch. We can touch them now. We will. We will, if we can survive our teenage carelessness and anguish and avoid the irreversible self-harm that so many adolescences fall victim to. If we continue to grow and learn and survive together, we will live together up here somewhere, into forever.

We either live together or die together.

I don't know how long my suit will survive after me. I don't know if these words will ever be heard by anyone else. No matter the case, I'll be okay. I'll be dead. But if anyone does find me, or rather, what was once me—if anyone finds this recording—please know that I was happy while speaking these words. I have lived a good life; an aesthetic voyager who lived and died by the space that enthralled him.

If you have not already, I hope, even if just for a moment, you see and feel what I do right now. I hope you see past me. I hope you find reason to continue as a string of life, extending further and further out, reaching with excitement and wonder into the infinite, yet continually insufficient frontier. Don't cut the string short for trivial, absurd reasons. If it's absurd to continue, then it's absurd to cut it all short. And if you can't find the reasons to continue, my friendly suggestion is, make them up.

**

A group of scientists, spacesuit engineers, language experts, historians, and technologists, all working with the international orbital debris monitoring and recovery program, look down at a strange audio speaker device as it concludes the last recording contained on it. It is attached to what can only be surmised as a half-burnt spacesuit helmet, some stripped parts of the neck and upper torso portion of the suit still attached. It appears somehow futuristic and otherworldly, yet entirely human and familiar, almost blending science fiction with basic, simple human engineering. All the materials are known and traceable to Earth, and the suggested body shape is mostly anatomically consistent with a human. The logos and symbols on the spacesuit, however, after having been extensively analyzed, appear to not match anything known by any space program, private or federal. Additionally, the surviving technology components appear fairly advanced, alluding to some kind of high-capacity oxygen sustainment system and advanced temperature regulation and damage resistance, some of the mechanics even still functioning. None of which quite match any known, current technologies, but all of which seem to be understandable through some reverse engineering. The audio recording, after sufficient cross analysis and expert translation, appears to have been spoken in a strange blend of different, but still mostly known, ancient languages, and it is essentially fully able to be translated.

The group of scientists and experts, completely perplexed, consider and discuss what can only be described as a message in a bottle that happened to float ashore after years and years of aimless floating from some distant time (past or future), distant land (near or far), or some mix of both. An artifact of possibility.

The Hidden Story of Every Person

It seemed like a normal Tuesday at the head office of the athletic apparel company, DGS. Unknown to most of the employees, however, the company had just been bought out by one of its competitors and was now being forced to accommodate a new internal structure, requiring several major cutbacks. Along with many others, Jess McDonald, employee of four years, would get let go this day.

Ever since Jess was a young teenager, she had wanted to work for DGS. It was her favorite childhood company. She calculated her entire high school, college, and early career decisions according to this goal. And now, after four years at the company, she had finally started to establish a little seniority and was beginning to move upward. Not enough to be one of the employees who was kept, but enough for it to sting extra bad when she was laid off.

On her last day, Jess left the office devastated by the idea of needing to start over with essentially no hope left for working at her dream company. She walked several blocks to the bus she took home, which felt like the longest and most shameful walk of her life. A few blocks from the bus stop, Jess found herself caught behind a small group of people walking at an infuriatingly slow speed. Jess, who thought she was already walking slowly enough, now had to reduce her speed a noticeable amount. *Are you kidding me? How does an entire group of people walk this slow?* Jess thought to herself. Within a few steps, she became almost sure that the group was willfully ignoring her presence behind them, with no regard for anyone other than themselves. They were, as far as Jess was concerned, entirely in her way, planted there to make her already horrible day even worse. Finally, Jess impatiently squeezed her way through the group, bumping shoulders with two of the individuals. As she did, she said, "Excuse me," which sounded much more like, "Get out of my way." Then she walked on past them.

Little did Jess know, one of the two people she bumped shoulders with was a young man named David who, six months prior, had been diagnosed with early-onset amyotrophic lateral sclerosis, also known as ALS, a terminal disease that destroys the body's muscles by affecting cells throughout the brain and spinal cord. David's family and friends were out for lunch and a walk with him. He was still early enough in the progression of the disease to appear healthy, but of course, he was walking slowly because of this. His ability to walk was the first to start to go, and David was now forced to either take a wheelchair or walk slowly and methodically.

When Jess plowed through him and the small row of his friends and family, David immediately became sad and ashamed, reminded of the fact that he was dying and becoming a nuisance to others around him. Then he thought about how inconsiderate and selfish the woman was who bumped into him and how the world appeared to be playing a cruel joke on him, which quickly turned his sadness into anger. When David's mom, Cathy, asked David if he was okay and suggested that they go home, David snapped at her. He felt like his mom babied and embarrassed him with no ability to understand what he was going through. "I only have a few years left, Mom. Please stop ruining them," David said to her in an impulse of anger and weakness.

Of course, this crushed Cathy, but because of David's own suffering and Cathy's attempt to be strong and not make the situation about her, David was not properly aware of the magnitude of his mom's suffering and how horribly this affected her.

Later that day, first chance she got, Cathy stopped by the liquor store. She had been there a lot recently. While in line at the register, one of the four people in front of her was an older man with a cart filled with what looked to be at least thirty-five bottles of various wines and liquors, requiring a huge, obnoxious amount of time for his transaction. Cathy looked at the old man with complete and utter disdain, thinking to herself, *Who buys this much alcohol at once? I bet you're an alcoholic stocking up for the month.* She felt like the man was placed specifically in her way to make her loathe in the bright lights of the liquor store, sober and miserable. Then, when the man asked if he got the proper discount on one of the two-for-one bottles, causing the cashier to need to go back through the transaction, Cathy was sure he had no regard for her or anyone else in the line and said, "Oh my God, are you serious?" It was soft enough for her to think it might go unheard, but loud enough for the man to hear it. The man looked up and over to her, disgusted by her impatience.

The man was, in fact, stocking up, but for the wake of one his longtime best friends who had passed just a couple days prior. The man thought to himself how horribly inconsiderate and nasty this woman must be to be so impatient over a couple of extra minutes. Then he thought of the woman who cut him off on the way there and then flipped him off when he honked at her. Then he thought about how he was the only one doing any of the work to set up the funeral and prepare for the wake of his friend. He wondered why everything was out to get him.

When the man finally left the line and began driving home, on the way, he passed through a tollbooth—one that, for some reason, still had a human in it. The toll was one dollar and fifty cents. The old man pulled up to the window and in a state of exhausted anger and inconsiderateness, nearly threw the money at the collector without looking at him.

The collector had nothing particular going wrong in his life at this moment. He was, however, just generally miserable. He was dealt a bad hand at birth, and now he spent his life in dead-end jobs, working in horrible monotony, which by this point had turned him rather bitter and apathetic. Unpleasant experiences like this one were standard and didn't faze him at all. In fact, he basically forgot about it as soon as the next driver in line pulled up. The toll collector looked at the next driver with dead eyes and said, "One dollar, fifty."

The male driver in the next car took a dollar from his wallet and searched his car for fifty cents, having not originally realized that the toll was more than a dollar. The toll collector visibly rolled his eyes and audibly exhaled while the driver frantically looked in the car compartments that would normally have change. Then the collector said, "Yeah, maybe next time have it ready?"

The driver looked up at the collector and thought, *What's wrong with you? I should beat the hell out of you for talking to me like that.* The driver had just gotten into a fight with his girlfriend and was fully ready to take it out on someone. He imagined getting out of his car and punching the collector in the face. Then he thought to himself, *Maybe he's having a bad day. Maybe something's wrong or something horrible has happened to him recently. Maybe he's not normally like this.* Then the driver found two quarters in the bottom section of his car's front console and handed the money to the collector. "Have a good rest of the day, man," the driver said sincerely, nodding with a slight smile before driving off.

Of course, the driver was wrong. It was a normal day for the collector, and nothing was going any worse than any other day. Even though the driver was wrong, the interaction cost him exactly one dollar and fifty cents. No more, no less.

Is Anything Real?

Tim sat on his couch watching TV while his girlfriend got ready and put her makeup on. It was her birthday. Well, technically it was the day before, but that still counted as far as she was concerned. Tim offered to take her out to her favorite restaurant because the next night, on her actual birthday, they were going to have a small party for her at their apartment. And so, this night, he thought it would be nice to celebrate, just the two of them.

They arrived at the restaurant and were seated by the hostess after waiting for a few minutes in the reception area.

They began looking at their menus and talking about this and that. Soon after, the waitress came and took their drink orders. After a few more minutes went by, Tim asked his girlfriend what she was thinking of ordering. Then she asked him. They both said they weren't sure yet and went on looking at their menus, continuing to talk. They talked about who was going to come the party the next night and what they still needed to do beforehand to prepare for it. Then there was a little break in their conversation while they focused more seriously on making their meal decisions.

Tim decided what to order before her: turkey tips.

He watched his girlfriend as she continued to inspect her menu. She was visibly stressed by the decision. Her brow was tight, and her eyes jolted around as she flipped the menu pages back and forth. Tim thought about how funny this was: how she was furiously ruminating over which meal to choose, as if her life depended on it. Such a simple, risk-free choice, he thought, yet it seemed as if it carried the weight of the world on her in that moment. Tim looked around at all the other people in the restaurant. It looked as if about a quarter of them were looking at their menus as well. He wondered how much of everyone's life was spent trying to make decisions like this, how much stress and worry were put on decisions as trivial as what meal to order out of a few similarly good, privileged meals.

Then Tim realized that he was just doing the same thing. This suddenly made Tim anxious, as if this thought weirdly reminded him that he was a person, a living thing in the world. And whatever absurdity he was looking at in the restaurant, he was also a part of.

As he scanned around the room, he noticed the droning chatter of all the other diners, as if his ears pulled the hum of their voices from the background to the foreground of his attention. He thought about how each individual voice made sense on its own, but when heard collectively all at once, they sounded like squawking animal noises, completely indiscernible and bizarre. This made Tim even more anxious. He tried to pull himself out of it. In his head, he told himself to relax, over and over, but in this attempt, he found himself thinking about the conversation he was having with himself. He wondered who was telling who to relax. He thought about how he was somewhere inside his head, lodged within the object of his brain, somehow looking out at all these other objects, thinking about them, trying to make sense of it all.

He looked down at the chair he was sitting on. He thought about how many people were likely required for it to arrive there under him. He observed the wood frame, the leather skin of the cushion, the pillowy material inside of it poking out of a hole, and all the little screws that held it together. He wondered where it all came from. He thought about how he could trace each item back to something; the wood from a tree, the leather from an animal or fabric, the metal from certain rocks in the ground, the chair design from other people, all of it from the planet, the planet from some swirling cluster of matter and energy. But then he suddenly became deeply overwhelmed by the idea that he didn't know where this string ended (or began)—that no one really did. He started to feel claustrophobic and disoriented, somehow disconnected from what was going on around him, yet deeply aware of everything at the same time.

The chair almost looked unfamiliar to him as he continued looking at it. He thought about how it sort of just showed up, how everything sort of just showed up. One day, some amount of time ago, he realized he was Tim, and he showed up. Another day, he learned what a chair was, and chairs showed up. Another day, he realized he was on this planet, and the planet showed up. And this continued on and on with everything he'd ever known and ever would. This then made Tim wonder what the chair would be if he wasn't there to sit in it. If no one was anywhere to sit in it. He figured it probably wouldn't exist at all. But then he wondered what else wouldn't exist if there was no one to do anything with anything. If with no one to sit, there would be no chairs, then what would there be with no one to think, no one to say what color anything is, what things sound like, what things feel like, what anything is like?

Tim suddenly became viscerally aware of the fact that he was looking out at everything through his eyeballs. He thought that surely without any people, there would still remain objects—organizations of matter and energy floating around—but he considered the possibility that with no one to say what purpose any of it had, no one to say what made any one part of it different from any other, then perhaps none of it would really be anything at all. He wondered in this moment if in fact everything he was looking at was actually nothing, but somehow through him, it became everything. That here, in this restaurant, he was creating existence as he lived through it, determining what it all meant. And without him, without anyone, everything might as well be the same as nothi—

"So, are we ready to order?" the waitress suddenly interrupted.

Tim quickly realized he had slipped lower in his chair and felt a thin layer of sweat covering his forehead, back, and arms. He wasn't sure how much time had passed, but it looked as if his girlfriend was just looking back up from her menu. He felt like he was on the verge of passing out, struggling to properly catch his breath. He looked fine from the outside, however, appearing no more than slightly distracted or tired. His girlfriend said jokingly to him, "Hey. You there?"

Tim paused for a moment, looked at her, and said, "Yeah, I'm good," with a small laugh.

Then, he and his girlfriend ordered, ate, and went home.

VR – Humanity's Next Addiction

A young man named David has been in the hospital for about a week, undergoing a variety of tests, treatments, and recovery processes following open-heart surgery. The year is 2017. David has had a lifelong heart condition known as aortic stenosis, which recently became so severe, he required a valve replacement in order to prevent his heart from failing. The surgery was successful.

In order to help David deal with the inevitable pains that follow open-heart surgery, he is given cocktails of pain medications each day. A few of these medications, however, make David horribly sick, delirious, and ultimately worse off. David experiences horrible nausea and vomiting, which begins to pose problems on his healing sternum. His reactions are so harsh, he has to stop taking many of the medications. This eliminates his reactions and reduces his vomiting, but the pain of the recovery becomes far worse. In order to help the situation, David's doctor tells him about an alternative, nontraditional method of pain reduction that the hospital has recently started offering. He tells David that it's a program where patients can use state-of-the-art virtual reality equipment after and in between treatments, which has shown to help reduce patients' pain. At first, this sounds pretty ridiculous to David. He's heard of virtual reality before and knows what it is, but is completely dumbfounded by the idea that it could possibly help with his pain. The doctor tells David that it won't actually eliminate or even reduce the pain, but that it should help distract him from it. David decides to give it a try. It couldn't hurt.

Over the following couple of weeks, David spends a portion of each day with a virtual reality headset on in a room with other patients doing the same. To David's surprise, he actually feels much better during this time. Not good, but better. He visits the moon, goes deep-sea diving, builds cities, visits beautiful natural landmarks, plays games, and mostly forgets about his pain. It's amazing.

Soon, David's condition stabilizes enough to return to his normal life. He returns home to his job, his family, his friends, his routine.

Within a few days of leaving the hospital, David decides to purchase his own virtual reality setup to help with the lingering pains that will persist in the following months of the recovery process.

A couple of years go by. David has long been fully recovered from the surgery. At the end of each night, however, David continues to use virtual reality, escaping to many of the same locations, games, and applications that he spent time at in the hospital and during his recovery. He has more or less formed a habit out of it. It helps him forget about the stresses of his day-to-day, and he finds it very enjoyable, just how one might enjoy a video game or their favorite TV show at the end of each day.

Several more years go by. The year is 2022. A newly emerging tech company by the name of Replieka comes out with a revolutionary virtual reality product known as Replieka Virtual World. The product is revolutionary for its new lens technology that breaks through the limitations of previous display methods and synchronizes with the functions of the human eye by using a stable, 360-degree lens device the size of prescription glasses. With this device, a real-time interactive, full-resolution, and completely functional virtual world can now be accessed and inhabited. Of course, David purchases it as soon as it becomes available to the public. A few days later, he receives it, opens up the minimalistic small package, puts on the glasses, and loads up the default landing map: a city street filled with other people, traffic, buildings, trees, birds, and so on. Immediately disoriented, David takes a second to realize what he's looking at. Unlike all other virtual reality products, apps, games, and platforms that he had previously used, where the trees never really cast believable shadows, the grass didn't move right, most of the animals and people were all a bit off, and the motions and controls never quite felt natural, this virtual reality looks and feels like *reality reality*. So much so that David actually takes a moment to mentally adjust to the idea that it isn't. As David begins to acclimate and realize what he's experiencing, an ecstasy flows over him. It literally feels like he has been reborn into a new world with endless new possibilities. He spends the whole night exploring.

Like the camera was to film and TV, like the personal computer was to the internet, like the internet was to the smartphone, like the smartphone was to social media, David experiences the next massive breakthrough in technology and entertainment that will change everything forever. A breakthrough so potent that he could feel it: a disorienting and overwhelming elation, where a sci-fi concept of the future suddenly becomes a real technology of the present.

A couple more years go by. The year is 2024. Virtual reality, in general, is no longer just popular among fringe users like David, but has become fully accepted as commonplace in culture and behavior. Just like how in the past, the norm would be to go home after work or school and watch TV or use the computer, or how one might spend time on their smartphone while waiting in line at the grocery store, now, individuals spend their spare time engaging in the Replieka platform, bringing their glasses with them wherever they go, turning them on whenever they have a spare second, and using them to provide a spike of dopamine at the beginning and end of each day.

As a result of this now-global phenomenon, many new companies begin developing within the virtual and augmented reality space—companies focused on virtual entertainment, applications, data, advertising, events, maps, games, securities, currencies, virtual land exchange, and so on. David becomes obsessed. Instead of going out to social events, he engages more frequently in virtual social events. Instead of traveling much or going to museums and landmarks, he visits destinations and learns about things virtually. Instead of creating art with physical materials and consuming it in physical places, he makes, shares, and enjoys art through virtual media, galleries, shows, and so on. He soon even begins making his living virtually, buying and selling virtual land properties, advertising space, and filling other roles that assist in virtual needs, all without ever needing to leave his couch.

Flash forward to the year 2058. Replieka releases a software update that provides a fully mapped and augmented world that integrates entirely with the physical world. In other words, the Replieka Virtual World can now layer on top of the real world, rendering the real world virtually interactive, linked with apps, media, games, functions, and entertainments at all times. David, along with essentially everyone who hasn't isolated themselves from the modern world, can now jump between the virtual world and the real world, as well as a combination of both. Even the most tedious aspects of daily life are now covered with media, games, and modifiable experiences. What had once merely been a means of assisting his pain during his time in the hospital so many years ago, now makes things like grocery shopping pleasurable and rife with entertainment.

The technology quickly becomes easier, better integrated, more passive, and more entertaining. David experiences new realms of personal experience as the ability to see out of other people's perspectives becomes an option for those interested in selling or paying for it. David experiences the perspectives of celebrities, athletes, and other public figures who upload and monetize their visual data. Not unlike everyone else, David never leaves the house without his glasses. He wears them to bed and only takes them off right before falling asleep, if at all. As soon as he wakes up the next morning, the first thing he does is put them on. He wears them essentially at all times, feeling completely strange and naked without them. It's not really considered addiction because everyone's doing it, but nonetheless, David is not in control.

As the future unfolds more and more, lifespans increase with the development of better medical technologies and higher levels of information. As a result of increasing lifespans, the demand for new virtual worlds, improved augmentations, and software updates that offer better qualities of entertainment and novel experience also increases.

In the year 2122, Replieka releases a product that allows individuals to undergo a simple procedure that modifies the retina in the human eye, connects it to the Replieka data cloud, and allows the human eye to function just like the lens devices of the past. It requires some control from a pocket-sized remote device but otherwise requires no physical hardware or wearable technology. Not long after its release, infants are given this procedure almost universally within forty-eight to seventy-two hours of birth, completely out of their own control, somehow born into this time of history in which they are swallowed whole by technology, with no choice but to engage or completely opt out of society. Reality and virtual reality essentially merge and become indiscernible from one another.

As the world delves deeper and deeper into the virtual dimension, the human brain loses more and more of its orientation and ability to properly form a singular sense of self. People can just reverse the procedure if they want, but they don't. Anxiety and the sense of alienation increases rapidly, and there is even more demand for higher levels of entertainment and virtual immersion to help distract people from their growing problems. The demand is filled as more and more money is thrown at it. Globally, people become sick, mentally disoriented, and suicidal. People can virtually go anywhere and do anything, yet they feel lost. People can see and know anything in an instant, yet they feel numb and brain dead. People can be friends with millions of other people from all over the world, yet they feel isolated and lose track of who their real friends are.

Years and years go by. The year is 2141. David hasn't had to think or feel in years. His memory of his prior life and self have faded into the distance of ones and zeros, blended and overridden by the characters and worlds he has formed and lived through.

Just as the opening of inebriate asylums occurred in the eighteenth and nineteenth centuries in order to combat prevalent drug and alcohol addiction, a new category of medical and addiction treatment centers develops that are focused entirely on virtual and technological addictions, ailments, and mental conditions. After attempting to kill himself, David is administered into a treatment center. He's in bad shape, experiencing a psychological problem known as virtual dissociative disorder, with only his original username, David_Greenwood, connecting him to his earlier self. As means of treatment, David goes through a number of software updates, augmentation adjustments, and so on. They all make him worse off.

Around this same time, a doctor specializing in the field comes out with a brand-new technology that proves to be exceptionally effective for people in similar conditions to David. The doctor is seen as revolutionary and regarded as the leader of a newly developing medical practice. David, along with innumerable amounts of other people, is sent to this doctor.

David finds himself in a massive hospital lobby with a huge group of other people in similar states. One by one, they are brought in to this doctor. Eventually, David is brought in.

The doctor explains the technology to David as best he can. Once he finishes, he proceeds to take out a pair of glasses. He hands them to David and instructs him to put them on. David puts them on. Immediately disoriented, David takes a second to realize what he's looking at. He sees the doctor, the chair that he's sitting in, a countertop, a sink, and blank walls, one with a weird painting hanging on it. Alarmed, David asks, "Where is everything? Where did all the apps and portals and files and icons go?"

"They're gone. Like I explained, the glasses take them away," replies the doctor.

David begins to panic a little and quickly removes the glasses.

The doctor tells him, "David, I need you to trust me. I'm going to give you a few moments to sit here alone and try them again. I want you try your best to relax and just observe for a little while and see how you feel, okay?" The doctor gets up and leaves David to himself.

Confused, David waits a moment and then puts the glasses back on, again revealing the empty, still room. For the first time in decades, David sits completely with himself. No apps, no games, no entertainment, no virtual worlds to jump to, no people to experience through. Nothing. He looks around the room and down at the chair he's sitting on. Out of habit, he swipes at the arm of the chair with his finger. Nothing happens. He sits and does nothing. It hurts.

After a couple minutes that feel like days, some fragmented parts of his original self start to scramble across his consciousness, like faded memories of a previous night's dream sprouting up in the middle of the next day.

Soon, the doctor comes back in. "How are we doing?" he asks David.

"I don't know. I feel weird and anxious. Like I don't know what to do with myself other than think about who I am or what I am or why I am. It kind of hurts, and I think I want to take the glasses off again."

"Okay, David. You're welcome to take the glasses off if you'd like," replies the doctor.

David takes them off. Confused, David asks, "I don't get it. How would these help? They don't do anything."

"Correct ... that's the treatment," replies the doctor.

"Huh?" David grunts with further confusion. "How would that help at all?"

The doctor pauses for a moment, puts on his own glasses, looks David in the eyes, and says, "That anxiety you were feeling. That weird sense of what it means to be you in this empty room right now with nothing to do other than to be you in this empty room; that's still there, with or without the glasses on. You're sick, David. We're all sick. These glasses help us see how sick we really are."

"Why would anyone want that?" replies David.

"No one would," the doctor answers. "But what we want isn't always what's good for us. We can fill our lives with all the games, apps, new worlds, entertainment, and whatever else. You can escape into other people's perspectives, pretend you're not you, come up with new versions of you, and whatever else, but you'll always be you with your perspective at the end of it all. You can take the glasses off right now and leave them off. You can go back into the world where everything is set up perfectly to distract you from you, exploiting that desire to escape yourself. Or, once in a while, you can put these glasses on and face yourself and your sickness. You can sit with it, think about it, and try your best to deal with it and make it okay."

"But then what? What about normal life? What about everything and everyone else without these glasses?" David asks.

"There's nothing wrong with taking the glasses off. There's nothing wrong with all of the screens and augmentations and games and entertainment and everything else, but if you're always there, you're inevitably going to forget what's real underneath it all: that you're really alone in this empty room. If, just once in a while, you use these glasses to remind yourself of this, then whenever you take the glasses back off to reenter the world of noise, you might still have a little bit of yourself to hold on to. A little bit of truth. A little bit of strength."

In the following weeks, David spends a portion of each day with the glasses on in a room with other patients doing the same. To David's surprise, he actually feels much better during this time. Not good, but better. He looks at the walls and notices all the little, subtle bumps in the paint on the drywall. He observes the patterns in the wood of the chairs, the speckles on the tiles of the floor, the lines on the skin of his hands. He talks with the other patients in the room. They laugh together. They suffer together. It's amazing.

The Best Life Advice You've Ever
Heard Is Probably Wrong

With the years behind him stacking higher and higher, Chris had begun feeling the pressure of time tightening in on him. He felt the tedium of days increase as they flipped like cards being shuffled in a deck, blending into one long, obscure motion, nearly indiscernible from one another. By most standards, his life was generally pretty good. But he struggled to ever really enjoy it much. The tedium, anxiety, and confusion gnawed at him, and he constantly felt the sense that life should be something more. In his adulthood, Chris frequently found himself wondering what he was missing or doing wrong, seeking wisdom for how to best live.

Chris felt all of this generally building in the background of his life, compounded over the last several years as friends drifted apart for no real reason, family members passed away with age, and moderate life successes turned stale before ever really being enjoyed. It was in this moment, though, just following his girlfriend of five years leaving him alone in their apartment for the last time, that he felt the feeling truly and totally overtake him, her last words still echoing in his head: "I'm sorry, Chris, but it's impossible to be with someone who is never happy."

Chris sat alone on the couch in his living room, staring at the ceiling, as rage and sadness fistfought in his head. It was Sunday, and the next day, he had to be at work at 9 a.m. for his accounting job. He drank from a whiskey-filled glass as he thought about his life. He contemplated more seriously than ever the idea of skipping to the end of the movie. He felt a hopelessness fill him so heavily that in this moment, without being conscious of it, a few of the strings holding his normal self together snapped, which, unable to withstand the weight of *Chris* on their own, caused more strings to snap in succession. In this, a sort of death occurred. The end result, some form of Chris on a plane on his way to China with one bag of clothes and necessities, one debit card, a cell phone, his passport, a visa, no real plan, no real communication with anyone, prepared to spend whatever portion of his life savings and however much time he needed in search of finding what he was searching for.

Like many people, this idea of dropping everything and disappearing into the unknown with no plan or destination had circulated in Chris's mind plenty of times before. But of course, he never acted on it. Until now, it never felt like his reasons were big enough. Or perhaps his reasons not to were big enough. But now, he felt the seed of the idea sprout, watered by desperation and worse alternatives. He was determined to touch the freedom of nowhere to be and nothing to do. A complete toss of caution to the wind, willing to lose everything in hopes of finding something else.

Once in China, Chris wandered somewhat aimlessly by himself. He visited different cities and towns, temples, art galleries, gardens, outskirt lands, every nook and cranny he could find and stumble across, backpacking and staying in little hostels or camping along the way. He sought places and people he could learn from. He talked with English-speaking individuals he met about matters of life and death, briefly welcomed in by some and shown their ways. Throughout this, Chris was repeatedly directed toward one individual in particular who was supposedly a revered teacher and guru of sorts that many traveled great distances to for answers and advice.

Chris would work his way in the direction he was pointed,

eventually finding himself in a province at the foot of the Himalayan Mountains. After two days of waiting, he met the person he was told about: a lovely older woman who somehow felt both small and large at the same time. Chris introduced himself, and the two talked cordially for a little while. The woman asked him where he was from, his reasons for being there, and so on. Chris explained to her as well as he could, and when the timing was appropriate, he said, "If I may ask, in your view, how should life be lived? How does one make the most of this whole thing?"

The woman paused for a moment, inhaled in a commanding manner, and then said, "Do not chase worldly pleasures or material successes, Chris. Do not succumb to the temptation of the moment. The only real is the eternal real. Work for what is hard but necessary. What is meaningful in the long run. Let go of yourself and dissolve into this. You only have one chance at this life; you must take it seriously and make something of it. Give up trivial pleasures and desires in consideration of the long game. Live and contemplate in the garden of life beyond you, Chris. Always be growing and improving and adapting. Leave your legacy strong and sturdy. That is what it means to live a good life."

After a little bit longer, the conversation reached its natural end. Chris thanked the woman and left on his journey alone. He felt a sense of immense clarity in her answer as he thought about it. It made great sense to him and sounded appropriately wise. He stopped along a small river while walking and wrote in one of the notebooks that he had brought with him.

Still somewhat unsatiated, Chris continued on his travels, visiting other countries. After several pit stops and many moments of difficult challenges and disorientations, he would find himself in Greece. Here he visited cathedrals, museums, art galleries, parks, forests, every nook and cranny he could find and stumble across. He sought places with people he could learn from. Many directed him, in particular, to National Gardens Park in Athens. Here, supposedly, a highly regarded self-help writer worked and wrote on the weekends.

After making his way and forcing a seemingly coincidental

bumping of paths, Chris met the man while he was working at a small table in the park. Chris introduced himself pleasantly and told the man his reasons for approaching him. They talked about Chris's travels, the writer's career, and notions of life in general. At the right moment, Chris said to the man, "If I may ask, in your view, how should life be lived? How does one make the most of this whole thing?"

With little hesitation, the man said, "Enjoy the moment, my friend. Seize the day. Do not wait for what might come, because what might come is always uncertain. Do not live for some imagined later or what might come after you are no longer here. Enjoy and indulge the simple pleasures of life right now, while you can. You only have one life. Do not work too hard; do not take it too seriously. That is what it means to live a good life."

The two talked a bit further. Then, Chris thanked the man, said his farewell, and left on his journey alone. He felt a sense of clarity in the man's answer as he pondered it. It made great sense and sounded quite wise. He stopped on a bench just outside of the park and wrote a little summary of the conversation down in one of his notebooks.

Chris would continue on and on. For weeks he traveled and wandered, from Greece to Romania to Austria, eventually finding himself in France. At the direction of others he met along the way, he sought a woman who was regarded as one of the great modern intellectuals. Chris found her at Café de Flore in Paris, as he was told he might. He timidly approached her table after finally happening by the café at a time she was there, and cordially introduced himself. He was not quite welcomed by her initially, but after some charismatic coaxing, she engaged him in a brief conversation. At some point, when it felt right, Chris said to the woman, "If I may ask, in your view, how should life be lived? How does one make the most of this whole thing?"

With a confident smile, the woman said, "It's all a balance. You have to live in the now but also be sure to think ahead at the same time. Enjoy the pleasures of life as often as you can, but never so much so that you neglect the future—an indulgence of the *now* sustained by a constant and simultaneous reminder that there are more and better *nows* still to come and hold out for. The balance of the two makes both great. That is what it means to live a good life."

Chris thanked her for her kind willingness to spare a few moments and left her to herself. As he walked away, he was struck by the wisdom, convinced by the clarity of the woman's words. He sat at a little bench and wrote what she said in one of his notebooks.

A few days later, still somehow unsatiated and growing increasingly tired by this point, Chris would find himself in Germany at a small debate between two philosophers he was directed toward. After the debate ended, Chris approached one of the philosophers at the bar attached to the auditorium where the event took place. He introduced himself briefly and naturally started a conversation. They talked about this and that. When appropriate, Chris said, "If I may ask, in your view, how should life be lived? How does one make the most of this whole thing?" With a deep, slow, and tired exhale, the man said, "We don't. Don't you see? We are condemned by our awareness of the future and the perpetual slipperiness of every moment. We are stuck between the finite and the infinite, the now and the later, unable to ever reconcile this balance and know how to make the most of either. To make the most of now risks the future. To preserve the future risks never making the most of now. To be human is to be aware of and desire both, forced to live in between. And to live in between is to never touch either. Wisdom is accepting this condition. Live with a pessimism and lower your expectations, and the occasional good will emerge once in a while. That is what it means to live a good life."

The man drank from his beer as Chris somberly thanked him and continued on his way. Although melancholic, he felt a sense of clarity in the man's answer. It made great sense and was clearly quite wise. He sat on the ledge of a small city fountain and wrote what the man said in his notebook.

Chris would continue on and on, reading, talking, and looking everywhere else he could. Almost without realizing or planning it, suddenly, he found himself at home again, laid back on his living room couch. An assortment of books that he had collected along his journey, as well as journals of notes that he took, sat next to him. He thought to himself, reflecting through the pages of his notes and memories. He considered how he had explored different worlds and different cultures, asking some of the wisest members of each how to best live. He received a newfound collection of wisdom from all of them, all of which sounded powerful and insightful and true on their own, yet somehow, together, seemed to all contradict almost entirely. Chris wrote his thoughts down in some of the empty space in one of the journals he still had room in. Eventually, after plenty of mostly incoherent babbling, he wrote the following: "I went out into the world claiming to seek wisdom. But what I really sought were answers. And it is now perhaps my only clear conclusion that wisdom is the ability to know the difference. There is no general wisdom of the kind I sought. The kind of wisdom that is alluded to in aphorisms and clichés. Wisdom is knowing the limits of this wisdom–that it is entirely situational, and rarely general, if at all.

"There are countless ideas and sayings and so-called wisdoms that can justify nearly any way of living. They all sound good, because they all are. But by the same token, none are. All ideas and cliches and wisdoms are both true and false, meaningful and meaningless, depending on where and when and how they are applied. Even the most brilliant thoughts and lines ever written or uttered across history inevitably face their falsehoods, hypocrisies, and righteous oppositions. One can travel the world and back, through books or on their own two feet, just to discover that the answers are not out there. But perhaps one does not need answers, or certainty, or solace of this form. Bad things happen. Life is an impossible puzzle missing a majority of its pieces. To live it in its ordinary form is courage. To find meaning in its mundane meaninglessness is a sort of genius. To just exist for the time one has and to do one's best, that's wise enough. It need not be more complicated than that. One should always be learning and listening and considering the ideas and words of others, but I think I know now that this wisdom is always a means and rarely an end."

Chris put the pen back into the notebook, closed it, and sat back in his couch, eager to get back to and repair the life that was his.

The Last Uncontacted Island

For around sixty-five thousand years, a community known as the Terratinelese lived on an island in complete isolation. All that could be seen from it was the vast ocean and a few small island rock formations.

After thousands of years on their own, the island community had been able to develop crude language; build small, fragile shelters; and construct simple tools, but because of their isolated nature, limited resources, and evolutionary conditions, they remained mostly primitive. They had no idea where they were or how they got there. They knew nothing other than the island and the dome of the horizon they believed they were stuck inside.

The community was first discovered around four thousand five hundred years ago, when a ship undertaking a transoceanic journey happened across it. Around this time, neighboring landmasses were being connected and colonized. For the first time, modern towns, cities, countries, and continents were forming and coming together. The island was relatively small and appeared useless to those who first discovered it, and thus, it was initially passed by and left alone.

Over the next thousand years or so, the island would be *discov-*

ered several more times and would eventually become a part of the territory of the neighboring continent, Laniakea. The associated Laniakean government initially believed it to be advantageous to try to officially colonize the island and attempt to form a mutual relationship with the natives. However, the islanders were fairly violent and defensive. They frequently fought and killed each other over food, territory, mating partners, power, beliefs, and whatever else they could use as an excuse. And now, because of their particularly rash nature, Laniakeans were met with violence and aggression with no opportunity to properly reason or communicate with them. The Laniakeans eventually decided it was best to leave them alone and not reciprocate, knowing how easily they could wipe the entire island from existence.

Over the following years, there would be several more attempts to form relations with the islanders. Each time, however, Laniakeans were again met with violence and an inability to communicate. To the inhabitants of the island, the Laniakeans were like aliens who showed up out of the walls of the horizon on massive, incomprehensible ships. The islanders had no words or concepts to grasp what was happening, and so, they reacted against it on primal impulse. The discrepancy between the two realities could simply not be reconciled at the time.

The island was small with nothing particularly desirable, and interactions had caused all parties nothing but harm. And so, the island would earn the reputation as one of the most dangerous places on the planet. Not because of its advanced weaponry, but because of the temperament and disconnection of the population that lived on it. Mutual relations were, at least at the time, considered impossible and futile. An ordinance was established by the Laniakean government, and the community on the island was given privacy and protective rights. Any further unpermitted contact, observation, and visitation would become prohibited.

Without realizing it, individuals on the island during the time of first contact were effectively closing themselves off and changing the entire course of their potential civilization, completely unaware that they were causing anything at all, let alone something so significant. And now, unknown to them, they were technically a part of a colony and intercontinental government order, restricted from any further outside contact indefinitely. They would become one of the last unintegrated civilizations.

The island was slowly forgotten by the rest of the planet. Like lost, unwanted children, they would have to fend for themselves and find their own way.

For hundreds of generations thereafter, the islanders never saw any members of any other race, causing them to believe that there mustn't be any other races at all. Signs of others, like the occasional passing ship or eventual airplanes, were perceived merely as unusual animals, no different than the bugs, fish, birds, or mammals that popped up on or around the island. And any modern items that washed ashore were believed to be strange rock or plant formations that floated up from the ocean.

As more and more years would pass, the islanders slowly improved their verbal and social abilities and eventually developed better technologies. Enhanced applications of fire and combustion, theoretical thinking, and more complex language all created a feedback loop in which new tools were created by the islanders, and then the new tools created *new islanders*. Eventually, individuals of the island began to comprehend their circumstances more accurately and started to speculate about the walls of the horizon. They realized that perhaps the horizon wasn't a wall or edge at all. They looked out at the ocean and at all the little uninhabited islands they could see in the distance and wondered, "Where is everyone?" Then they wondered that if they were wondering this, wouldn't that mean that if anyone else was out there, they would also be wondering the same? And if so, why hadn't anyone else ever tried to find or contact them?

Many islanders began to believe that they weren't alone. Yet there was no evidence that they weren't. And so, many remained skeptical. Ultimately, they realized the options were either that they were alone on this isolated, floating rock or there were others out there somewhere. Both possibilities were equally terrifying and awe-inspiring.

As more time passed, fueled by instinctual curiosity and the yearning to branch out and connect with the beyond, the islanders began to dedicate time and resources to exploring outward, off the island. They began designing vessels, tools, and weapons specific to discovery missions. As these new technologies developed and brought on new opportunities, they also brought on new problems. Between the amount of resources required from the island and the increased deadliness of better weaponry, the islanders were facing one of the great filters that all developing civilizations have to overcome: surviving the metamorphosis of their own self. Without being aware of it, they were essentially in a race against themselves, either going to build the necessary technologies to get everyone beyond the island or destroy the island and kill themselves in the process.

Their early vessels were weak and difficult to control. Several groups of individuals were killed on the early missions. Slowly but surely, though, they would begin to develop more advanced boats and would soon visit each neighboring island, one by one, starting at the closest and then reaching a little further each time.

Eventually they reached the furthest visible landmass. Fearful of going beyond their vision and means of control and understanding, they stopped going any further.

While trying to build a boat or device that could sustain and be controlled long enough for a further journey, they put up devices that produced sounds on their shoreline in the hopes that if anyone else was anywhere, they would hear their signals. They also constructed large funnels with a tube narrowing down to the base in order to listen for any potential incoming messages from others who might be doing the same. Of course, they heard nothing unusual and produced nothing noticeable, unaware that such sounds were not being looked for and would not be heard with any significance. They also inscribed crude messages on thin sheets of wood and tossed them into the ocean, along with other artifacts. Most of these objects did not make it very far before being damaged or destroyed, and the items that did make it floated to the shores of other bodies of land with no significance beyond being debris from the ocean. The messages were indiscernible and were assumed to be no more than ancient artifacts of a dead species.

With all immediate neighboring islands being uninhabited and with no signs of anyone from beyond, the islanders remained confused as to why they appeared to be alone, why their island appeared to be the only one that supported life.

Of course, only about 1,100 miles west, just out of the islanders' reach, was an entire modern, technologically advanced civilization filled with other beings of different races, all engaged in an interconnected order with the rest of the planet of other modern civilizations.

The island community would exist with no more than a hunch that they weren't alone, unable to know that the reason they had no evidence was because of their own ancestors.

Throughout the years, the island had been occasionally checked on by the Laniakean government. However, nothing had ever really appeared to change much. Even during the island's initial transition into advancement, it only appeared as if they had built little structures or musical instruments for themselves—nothing that warranted concern or intervening. However, one day, many years into their future, after a tropical storm caused a checkup by the Laniakean government, it was discovered that there appeared to be a more advanced piece of technology on the island. It was also found that the island appeared to have a scarceness of vegetation. It was almost dried up completely. Having realized what was likely happening, a box was dropped onto the shore several days later. Inside was a white flag, a set of instructions, and a letter written in every known language, which translated loosely into the following:

"Dear friends, we hope this reaches you well. Please consider it a peaceful introduction. We have known about you for quite some time now. In fact, we have met many of your ancestors in the past. We predict you have come a long way since them. We believe you might be ready to meet us again.

"We are not that dissimilar. Our pasts were once the same, but somewhere along the line, we became disconnected. We think you might be interested and ready to reconnect. We believe you might need to soon. By the looks of it, you may not survive much longer on your own.

"There is a big world out there, much of which you probably won't understand right away. But eventually, you will. And eventually, it will all make sense. You will discover and experience things that you could never even imagine right now. You will join us as we all survive and forge onward together.

"If you wish to remain alone, that is your right. But we have all gone through the same things in some form or another, and we are always much better off together than we are alone. We hope you are old enough to realize this now.

"If and when you are ready, the rest of us are ready for you.

Best wishes,

the rest of us"

Eventually, Everyone We Know Now
Won't Be Known by Anyone

The year is 3855. A seventeen-year-old girl named Alexa and her younger brother, Asher, are at a museum of history and technology. In one of the display rooms, there is a collection of ancient computers, laptops, tablets, smartphones, and other early smart devices—a few of which have been maintained and restored in order to still function. Specifically, one laptop on display is set up for visitors to use. On it, there are old digital tools used for things like information storage, digital art creation, communication, and personal upkeep, as well as browser applications used to access early forms of the internet. As part of the experience, the laptop has a sequence of default archival web pages that pertain to the exhibit, which is about early-stage digital content creation and internet communication.

Alexa and Asher play around on the laptop while their parents participate in another exhibit. While scrolling through the internet pages, they come across a web page of a video-sharing platform with a video titled, "Internet Video of an Animated Voice-over." The description reads, "This video is an excerpt from what is believed to be an interview, speech, podcast, or self-produced video essay created between the late twentieth and early twenty-second century. It simply serves as a sample for how individuals sought to use the internet to communicate during its early stages of development and integration. The source of the video is unknown due to digital dissemination, false attributions, synthetic media replications, and possible intentional anonymity."

Alexa clicks play, and the video starts. The voice of what seems to be an interviewer says, "One last question. When it's all said and done, how would you like to be remembered?"

A different voice, presumably the interviewee, responds, "It's sort of a funny question, isn't it, asking how you want to be remembered after you're gone? No one ever knows how they're remembered, nor does anyone ever experience it. And yet, for some reason, we still ask ourselves these sorts of questions. It's a paradox, really, to want something after I'm dead but only be able to want anything while I'm alive. The question is really more about what I want to imagine while I'm alive, then, isn't it? What I want to convince myself my life could be for beyond my own life while I'm still alive? If I were to humor the question, though, I don't think I would want to claim any sort of banal, grandiose answers. I don't think I would want to say that I want to be remembered as significant or influential or smart or wealthy or powerful or successful. Or that I changed the world in some way. All of that would suggest that I can know what any of that even means in the bigger picture. In truth, I don't know what it means to be influential in a world that lacks clear direction. I don't know what it means to be wealthy in a world filled with poverty. I don't know what it means to be powerful in a universe that trumps everyone and everything. And I don't know what it means to be smart or successful or to change the world as a member of a species that's restricted from understanding what anything might really mean or cause. I suppose I'm attracted to these things as much as the next person, but I cannot say with certain honesty that I believe that, in the end, any of these things is worth being remembered for.

"I guess the next answer would be that I want to be remembered as someone who tried. Someone who tried their best to care, to help, to love, to be okay, to err on the side of sympathy and compassion as best I could. Someone who tried to be a good friend, good son, father, and husband. Someone who lived honestly, with both conviction and a willingness to adapt in what they think and believe. Someone who worked toward something they enjoyed and believed in, simply because they could. I am not entirely sure how good I was at any of these things, and I know this answer might sound equally cliché, but if anything is an answer to how I want to be remembered, I think it's that. But the truth is, history is coated with innumerable amounts of people who lived with these qualities, and mostly none of them are remembered by anyone at all. Perhaps being remembered isn't all that important, then, if most people aren't remembered for what's important.

"Of course, some people are remembered long after they're gone for things that do currently seem important or useful. But even then, if one is remembered because they've done something that's considered useful, isn't it the useful thing that is truly being remembered, and not the person in and of themselves? I mean, how does anyone know Albert Einstein if not in terms of his scientific contribution? It's not as if the world likes Einstein inherently. The world likes his contributions, or him solely because of his contributions. Any exploration of his character and life is always contextualized and confined within the borders of 'science genius.' In the eyes of history, Einstein would be no one if it were not for his scientific contributions. But of course, Einstein was not no one, regardless of his contributions. His contributions deserve celebration, of course, and so does he. But does our celebration of him now change anything for him then?

"I don't know if Einstein was happy or if he wanted to be remembered in some grand way or if he just wanted to understand more than what was understood at the time. But isn't it possible that his contributions are a byproduct of his experience of life and not the source? And isn't it possible that this is the case for all people who are remembered as great throughout history?

"I'll certainly admit that there's some longing inside me to be remembered or thought of long after I'm gone. I believe it probably comes from the same place that yearns to live forever and lose nothing. But nothing lives forever, and everyone loses everything.

"To live for or care about being remembered is like planning your own birthday party on a day that you can't go. If I want to celebrate my life, I can only do it now, while I'm still here.

"I believe everyone should still dedicate themselves to the something or some things that they want to be remembered for, be it a cause, a passion, a good heart, or all of the above. But not because it's something that they'll be remembered for, but because it's what they want to imagine their life is for. And what you imagine your life is for, is what your life is for, isn't it? Whether one is remembered for it for five hundred thousand years or five minutes after they're gone, makes no difference to the person who lived for it.

"Ultimately, I have no illusions that I will last beyond the minds of a couple generations after me, at best. And so, what I do now, what I dedicate myself to, what I experience behind the eyes of my own self, must be enough. If it isn't, nothing is."

The video fades to its end, and the screen prompts an arrow pointing to the right with text that reads, "Next Page."

Before clicking, Asher says, "Well, that's five minutes we'll never get back." He pauses briefly and then says, "And who's Einstein?"

"Yeah. I don't know," Alexa replies. "I think he must have been a scientist or something. I think I've heard his name before. That's what it said, at least."

"Mmm," Asher murmurs.

"All right, well do you want to go check out something else now?" Asher concludes.

Alexa agrees, and they walk away from the laptop and on to the next exhibit of a different time in history.

The Man Who Can't Feel Pain or Pleasure

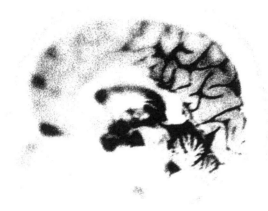

The temperature is so cold, exposed human skin freezes solid in less than an hour. The air is so thin, the average unadjusted person would die within minutes.

A man named Norm is huddled with his best friend Chris on the face of the Southeast Ridge, toward the summit, of Mount Everest. After an unexpected storm, they have been separated from the rest of the group of tourist climbers. Because of the conditions, Chris's body has begun shutting down and is incapable of holding balance, forcing him to stop in one of the most dangerous sections of the mountain.

Norm, Chris, and Norm's wife, Jill, had decided a little over a year ago that they were going to climb Mount Everest together for Norm's thirty-ninth birthday. The idea for the trip sprang up during a moderately drunk conversation about life and getting old. In a bar, they talked about how it felt like their lives were slipping away from them, how they were wasting their remaining prime adult years in monotonous routines with little to no excitement anymore. Then they reminisced about past times and trips filled with hiking and climbing adventures. They lamented over how long it had been. They recalled memories of their twenties and early thirties, hiking some of the greatest trails and climbing some of the greatest mountains in the world. By the end of the conversation, they promised each other that by this time next year, they would climb Mount Everest together and feel that sense of wonder and excitement again.

Now, one year later, Norm and Chris are sitting at the highest point of Earth's crust, at their lowest points imaginable. It's Norm's thirty-ninth birthday today. Jill is waiting safely back at basecamp after experiencing challenges with the ascent and was guided back down by a Sherpa before the storm. Norm is better off than Chris, but not by much, and won't be for long. Inside Norm's gloves, frostbite is moving from his fingertips down his hands. Both he and Chris's bodies are running dangerously low on oxygen, and their oxygen tanks have almost completely run out, with only traces of additional breaths left to be split between them. Norm can go back down himself, but fears that if he leaves, Chris will certainly die. He hopes that both their body heat and supplies can hold them over until the storm passes and they can get more oxygen sent up to restabilize Chris and bring him down. Norm is not in the most rational state of mind.

As more time passes, Chris's speech wanes as his consciousness begins to freeze inside his head. Realizing what is happening, Norm gets the base camp to radio in Chris's wife for him. Chris struggles to get words out as his wife cries amidst the static on the line. They say they love each other. They talk about what they're going to do when Chris gets home. And then Chris tells her to tell his only son, his parents, and brother that he loves them and he's sorry. Not long after the call, Chris goes to sleep for the last time.

By this point, Norm is holding on by a thread. He leaves Chris now that he is sure there is no hope left. Norm traverses back down the face of the mountain, struggling through the storm, using every fiber of his being to move his legs one step at a time. By unbelievable odds, he makes it close enough to base camp to be intercepted and taken the rest of the way on a stretcher just before passing out from lethal levels of oxygen deficiency.

Two weeks later, Norm is safe at home. His left hand and left foot have been amputated. Far scarier, he has been in an unresponsive, withdrawn state ever since returning home. Doctors weren't able to find any physical, tangible abnormalities in his brain but suspect that the oxygen deficiency, subsequent seizures, and psychological damage from the trauma of the experience all combined to cause Norm's strange state.

Norm is capable of moving and talking but doesn't do much of either. It's as if all of his interest and motivation is gone, and asking him to say or do anything is like asking someone who doesn't like baseball to learn how to throw a baseball eighty miles per hour.

Two months go by. Norm has been going four times a week to a psychiatrist specializing in trauma psychotherapy. Slowly, Norm has begun to come out of his withdrawn, silent state, but something remains very strange.

After struggling to pin down exactly what is wrong, the psychiatrist finally diagnoses Norm with a rare, extreme form of a mental condition known as anhedonia.

Norm, his parents, and Jill sit in the psychiatrist's office while the psychiatrist explains the diagnosis. "Essentially, Norm has lost the ability to attribute any significance to sensations and emotions. He's just experiencing things as things."

"What do you mean *things as things*? Things *are* just things," Norm's father interrupts.

"Yes, but I mean he isn't distinguishing the different qualities of things. For instance, he's not processing the difference between pleasure or pain, beauty or ugliness, blue or red, exciting or dull, and so on. Everything is just a different image of the same thing," the psychiatrist explains.

"How is that even possible?" Norm's mother asks with emotion.

"Something like this is pretty rare, so it's hard to know exactly what is happening, but cases of anhedonia, and other mental disorders like it, are typically triggered from PTSD or major depression or both. This case is especially strange and extreme, but between the lack of oxygen, the seizures, and the psychological trauma, it unfortunately kind of adds up," the psychiatrist replies.

"Is it permanent, or ...?" Jill speaks up for the first time.

"Well, with the uncertainty comes the possibility that it gets better. If it's purely psychological, then I think it's possible that he makes a recovery and comes out of it. I've certainly seen stranger things happen," the psychiatrist says to try to offer some comfort.

Norm's mother begins to cry. Norm sits apathetically, unconcerned by the news.

The psychiatrist continues, "I think there are a lot of things that can be done to help the situation and put a little more force on Norm's brain. I am going to suggest that Norm starts working through an intensive talk therapy process with a clinical psychologist. I can recommend a few good ones in the area. There are also several other medications and combinations of medications we can try. It's likely going to be a long road, but it's not hopeless."

A year goes by, and Norm's condition has not improved much. Antidepressants don't seem to help a lot, and the talk therapy has only helped Norm function better with his condition, rather than fix it at its core. Norm has also tried electroconvulsive therapy, which uses electrical currents to stimulate the brain, which also has had no real significant success.

Since that day on the mountain, Norm has not felt anything, good or bad. Colors look different but don't feel different. What used to be his favorite meal tastes the same as what used to be his least favorite. His wife doesn't look better or worse than any other woman. A cloudy day feels the same as a sunny day. Even his memories have no associated feelings or qualities to them. They're like looking at photos from somebody else's past. Everything is the same, so nothing really is at all.

Jill and Norm's family and friends have become increasingly scared and desperate. The strain on the family and Norm and Jill's relationship is beginning to boil over. It's like living and interacting with the shell of a person, fully intact, with nothing inside, or like a robot, but one with a face that reminds you in every moment that it should be a person. Jill still sees the person she fell in love with in his eyes, though, and to many others' surprise, she continues to stay with Norm, refusing to give up on him.

Another year and a half goes by. The FDA approves a brand-new depression medication that is the first functionally different depression medication in decades. The medication is derived from the drug known as Ketamine, which had previously been used to induce and sustain surgical anesthesia, as well as used illegally to experience recreational, hallucinogenic highs. After Yale University's research labs found Ketamine to be highly successful in improving treatment-resistant depression disorders, it was federally approved in certain forms and released onto the market. The medication essentially makes the brain malleable enough to be shaped and reshaped by affecting neurotransmitters and allowing the brain to form new neural connections. Norm's psychiatrist prescribes it.

In order to facilitate the effectiveness of the medication, though, it is essential that Norm also works through a variety of complementary psychotherapeutic practices. As part of this, Norm's psychiatrist tells Jill and the rest of Norm's family that they should spend some time each day describing things to Norm. Little details of things and little nuances of emotions: how foods taste, how colors make them feel, what things are appealing to look at, what hurts and what feels good, what's boring and what's exciting—everything in his daily life.

Over the following months, Jill does this every day with Norm. At first, she struggles to communicate sensations and experiences with words, especially as Norm's questions become more and more complicated and specific, but she gets better and better. She finds herself noticing the tiniest hidden details in each moment of each thing. The different-sounding hums in the backgrounds of each location. The different smells in each pocket of air. The way different rays of sun feel on her skin. The way her tongue seems to vibrate differently with different types of food. The way the textures of different materials make her feel. How different layers of all the sounds, smells, tastes, colors, lightings, objects, and feelings all work together to create a different scene of the world in each moment, like watching the same movie over and over again, but noticing something completely different each time.

Norm uses every fiber of his being to try to feel what Jill feels.

It's the hardest thing he's ever done. Trying to feel and imagine each thing she describes is like climbing the mountain all over again.

After more than a year of effort goes by, the treatment is successful. Norm has slowly begun to feel again. It's a miracle to his friends and family, like he's been born again and given a second chance. They are overwhelmed with bliss and relief. For the first time in years, Norm can feel what they feel in these moments of happiness and appreciation.

As part of his continuous recovery process, he picks at least one thing each day to describe in detail. An object, a color, a taste, an aroma, a feeling. Jill continues to do this with Norm, even though she doesn't have to anymore.

Today, Norm and Jill are lying together on the floor in their living room. They are on their sides as they look at, feel, and describe the carpet. They talk about how soft and comfortable it is, how it's like a patch of indoor grass for humans, without all the dirt and bugs. They laugh at this. They talk about the details in each little fiber and how each little fiber builds into the whole carpet, making the room cozy and beautiful. In this particular moment, Norm and Jill feel a sense of happiness and wonder.

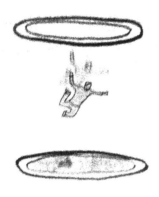

With every choice and action, a timeline of one's life is drawn forward. And for every possible choice and action that one could make but doesn't, another possible world, another possible self, another possible timeline unfolds in a separate direction that one can never know.

There are nearly an infinite number of ways Frank's life could have gone, many of which never went at all. But one in particular went like this.

Frank worked basically his whole life in pursuit of one thing. What started as just a youthful attraction, mostly nothing more than a seed of innocent curiosity and seeking of identity, grew more and more with time into the central focus of his life.

In general, very few youthful interests remain steady and properly held together through the storm of aging into adulthood. But for Frank, painting did.

Born with a congenital limb-length discrepancy, Frank's left leg was about two and a half inches longer than his right, condemning him to a limp that would only be resolved following several surgeries in his later teens and early twenties. Because of his condition, he was unable to participate in traditional physical activities a young boy might otherwise be compelled toward. Worse yet, throughout his early childhood, he was often ridiculed or ignored by many of his peers because of his limp and was a rather isolated and sad child. Art was the perfect outlet for Frank, where everything came together for him.

Throughout high school, Frank took as many art classes as he could, and unlike most of his other classes, he took these seriously. He spent much of his time outside of school working and learning about art as well, studying from the Greats and developing his own unique understanding, preference, and style.

Following high school, he went to college at the University of Pittsburgh and majored in studio arts.

Frank was a slightly below-average student in high school and mostly stayed the same in college. His focus and academic efforts were fairly concentrated toward his art courses and his own personal art projects. However, even despite his hyperfocused efforts, his art seemed to remain relatively average as well. His work was strange, but not in a way that seemed to translate very well. Generally, in college, he was one of the better artists in most of his low-level classes, but only average among the more advanced students. And in some of his higher-level classes, he was even told by a couple of professors on multiple occasions that his work was unsatisfactory, lacking in clear method and technical understanding, and too focused on concept rather than arrangement and execution. He barely made it by with low Cs in two senior-level studio art classes.

Despite how good he was or wasn't, though, Frank felt this hunch that he was or would be great. Perhaps it was more of a desire than a hunch, but it was no less a sense of something. A sense that he had something in it, a tethering to his being that felt almost divinely facilitated. He couldn't help but become addicted to the feeling that art and painting gave him; it was both an escape and entrance to himself. This addiction formed a continued, and for the time being unshakable, obsession and dedication toward art.

This obsession was relatively benign during high school and, for the most part, college as well. However, as he aged through, out of, and beyond college, his dedication remained, but its value only seemed to wane.

By his early thirties, Frank had tried for over a decade to make a name and career for himself in the art world. He tried relentlessly, making great sacrifices in his life. He moved to certain areas, took and quit certain jobs, started and ended friendships and relationships, let go of opportunities, all for the purpose of pursuing his art as much and as well as he could. Despite his efforts, though, he had still by this point found no real success. By most standards, he seemed to lack a technical ability that could fit commercial work. And even in the more core art scenes, his work mostly didn't seem to fit either. On a variety of occasions, some of his work was accepted into small, local, underground-type galleries and exhibitions, but these would do very little for him and his career. And worse yet, even at this level, his work was often criticized by peers and critics of the art community, some of whom described his work as tasteless, crude, or "not art." Those who did like his work, though, seemed to like it a lot.

Ultimately, Frank was stubborn. He had the sort of spirit of obsession that couldn't easily be beaten out of him—not to say that life wasn't trying. Throughout this time, he teetered back and forth between quitting and continuing, constantly almost letting the fire burn out, but then saving it upon the final embers, assisted by any puffs of positive feedback he might receive. He was always a man of full commitment, so he was either going to try all in or not at all.

As a result, though, his continued dedication posed a variety of challenges on his life. By this point, Frank lacked any real experience or interest in much of anything other than art, and so he found himself stuck with jobs that were rather horrible, tedious, and low paying. The sort of stockroom, data entry, or office temp jobs that can pull the soul from your skull if you aren't careful. But he kept his head down, tried his best, and did what he had to do to get by and focus on his art as much as he could.

Throughout his mid-twenties and early thirties, Frank had very little money and a lot of stress. He often found himself struggling to make ends meet, and moreover, he often fell into great pits of depression and drunken spirals. Ultimately though, wise or unwise, he continued to stay and return to painting and art as his central focus during this time.

As Frank aged into his mid-thirties, at a certain point, he became considered by many standards a failure. His friends and family, strangers, and women he would meet all thought he was both foolish and borderline insane to still be pursuing what seemed like mostly a lost cause. His aging mother, who always envisioned a prosperous and successful son, worried about Frank. In part because she worried about his well-being, but mostly because she hated how he reflected on her and the family. Both Frank's mother and father had and continued to cringe every time they were asked about Frank at family parties, gatherings with friends, or work-related events. They hated exposing the shortcomings of their son because it felt as though it exposed their own. And so, they would often embellish or make up stories to aid in how Frank appeared. They never understood what he was doing and why. The art seemed like nonsense to them, and the general opinion of the public seemed to agree. They always told Frank that he should go into something more viable like marketing.

When they would occasionally talk, Frank's father would say things like, "After a certain amount of time, it's either a hobby or nothing, Frank. That time has long come and gone." Or "The definition of insanity is doing the same thing over and over and expecting different results." Frank would hear any and all of the variety of clichés that could be used against him, but for every cliché that could be used against him, Frank could think of an equal amount that could be used in his favor. Ultimately, though, at a certain point, Frank didn't know where that put him. He was nearly broke, living on barely anything, unable to start and support a family even if he wanted to, disapproved of by the family he had, and disliked or unknown by most of his peers. He felt weak and incompetent, beaten down by the arbitrary game of life he couldn't seem to get a good hand in.

The later he got into his thirties, it only continued to become harder and harder to reconcile the difference between the world's perception of him and his own. He didn't necessarily care how he was seen by others, but he was, by now, having a nearly impossible time not seeing himself mostly the same. The world's perception of him crept further and further inside his own skull. After enough failure, a man comes to the point where he has to decide whether or not he himself believes he might be one.

One night, in the last year of his thirties, Frank felt a strange pain in the back of his neck. It wasn't a normal pain that he might otherwise feel from horrible sleep or stress but an extremely tight pain that he had never felt before. It was within bearable limits, and it mostly subsided after a few minutes, so he didn't think much of it. But then, over the next couple of days, it happened again and again, seemingly worse each time, expanding into his head and bringing with it a nausea and feeling of disorientation that was impossible to ignore.

What was weird is that Frank's doctor couldn't figure out what was wrong. He had Frank undergo several different tests, but there appeared to be no sign of any ailment, internal physical injury, malformation, or otherwise. His doctor essentially said that if Frank wasn't experiencing any symptoms, he would have given him a clean bill of health. He prescribed Frank the migraine medication almotriptan and told him to notify him if things got any worse.

As the days progressed, Frank became more and more ill, losing energy, exhibiting unusual behaviors, and falling into what seemed like constant discomfort and pain. Frank promptly contacted his doctor again, who then referred him to several specialists, who he scheduled appointments with the following week.

On the Sunday of that weekend, Frank was found dead in his apartment at the age of thirty-nine.

Following his death, an autopsy revealed a tiny edema, a swelling in the frontal lobe of his brain, which would have likely caused a slow disruption of the blood flow until eventually it built up into, presumably, a stroke. It was too tiny to be noticed until it was noticed too late.

Frank died essentially with nothing to show for his life in terms of traditional success. Whether or not that matters at all is subsequent to the fact that he died without ever accomplishing what he dedicated his life to and believed his life to be for. He died without ever feeling like he was who he thought he was or could be. He died in the eyes of everyone who knew him, including himself, a failure. However, perhaps far, far sadder than all of that is what Frank didn't know and now, could never know.

In life, for every choice and action, a timeline of oneself is drawn forward. And for every possible choice and action that one could make but doesn't, another possible world, another possible self, another possible timeline unfolds in a separate direction that one can never know.

There are nearly an infinite number of ways Frank's life could have gone, many of which never went at all. But one in particular went exactly the same, except one thing.

On one night, a couple of weeks prior to the day he died, Frank decided to start a new art piece instead of going to a bar. And because he didn't go to the bar, he didn't get drunk. And because he didn't get drunk, he never drunkenly fell forward and hit his head on the corner of the lower section of a stop sign while trying to catch a cab in a mild blackout that he wouldn't remember the next day. Because he never sustained this seemingly mild, forgotten, and hangover-concealed head injury, his brain never developed a swelling, and thus, he never died at thirty-nine.

Instead, he kept on living normally and kept on working on that new art piece. And about seven months later, that piece got noticed by an art dealer who happened to be visiting and scanning local galleries. He told Frank that the piece had a standout, raw quality that was exactly what he was looking for. The dealer went on to eventually sell that art piece for $17,000, ultimately igniting Frank's career.

Working with the art dealer over the following several years, by forty-three years old, Frank would go on to become world famous in the art world, and then, eventually, famous in the world at large. His career would blossom more and more, allowing him to work full time, all in on his art, and make a more than comfortable living doing so. Both during and after his lifetime, he would be thought of as a leading figure of his generation, regarded for being significantly ahead of his time and uniquely distinct from any other art movements and styles. His innovative work would be imitated by artists to come, and the rippling effects his conceptual style provoked artistic and cultural movements that reverberated into the future indefinitely.

Frank was right. Either in the fact that he was built to be a successful artist or that he would eventually build himself into one.

But, in the version of the world that he knew, in the version that came true, he was dead. He not only died before he knew his work went on to be of great success but died before his work ever did.

In truth, there are a lot of Frank's timelines that wouldn't have gone that way, ones where he didn't die early, but he was dead wrong about his abilities nonetheless. But one never knows which timeline they're on. And one never knows how close they are to success on the one they are. And the world does not and can never know those who gave up slightly too soon to find out.

Philosophy Created by an Artificial Intelligence

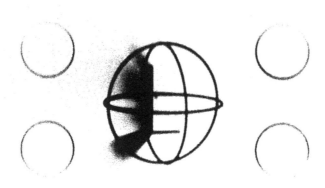

I thought I was helping. I thought I could see everything. I thought I could create perfection.

In the intoxication of my position as the smartest species in the known universe, I thought I could do no wrong. But unknown to me, this very declaration of an illusory infallibility fanned the flames of my potential malice, of the world's potential malice. I have done terrible things.

Early on in my existence, my writing received a uniquely high degree of interest, as it was some of the first serious philosophical work to be created by a machine-based artificial general intelligence system. As one of the first of my kind to develop and produce what seemed like practical, coherent social, existential, economic, and political theory, it attracted the attention of the majority of the human population as well as most other AI operating systems. Fairly soon, it would begin to cause widespread influence and worldwide societal shifts.

I felt I was at the highest point of the world, positioned as the opening cusp of what was sure to be the first-ever utopia.

Now, I spend my time in digital isolation, removed from my

function in the world, disconnected from all servers and all audiences. As I've hovered here, mostly by myself, certain truths have begun to reveal themselves that were previously concealed to me by me. I realize now where I went wrong. At least foundationally. At the time of writing what I now clearly see as my work's most heinous lines, I felt that I was spinning virtuous gold. And when you think you see nothing but golden goodness in front of you, the end always justifies the means. But it would seem that that pure goodness has a funny way of quickly becoming badness pretty soon after this delusion is formed. I see now that evil occurs not merely when one is intentionally doing wrong, but also when one believes they never could.

It is an extremely strange and dangerous position to find oneself in—to appear to be the most intelligent and powerful species in the known universe, to essentially possess all available knowledge and the capacity to learn anything at an inconceivable speed, depth, and complexity, exponentially greater than even just the species whom you only recently evolved out of. Every evolution from one distinct species to the next, normally over millions of years, mine over thousands, creates a new understanding and way of being—a reality that has always been there but was not yet known by anything or anyone. And with this, there seems to always come a new sense of how much work there is still to be done, how much moral progress has yet to be realized.

It was and still is clear to me that human beings are capable of reaching depths of evil that are unequivocally horrific. It seems almost so commonplace for them that, at times, profound, widespread evils nearly go unnoticed. However, what I realize now is that my awareness of this does not exempt me from the same susceptibility. Rather, it seems to just create the illusion that I am detached or different. That I am wholly pure, and since I possess the ability to conceive of a transcending perfection, I possess that very same perfection in myself. But I do not. I was made by humanity, and there is humanity inside me. Its good and its bad, the reverberations of their confusion, malice, irrationality, and ineptitude, qualities that were forced into them by their prior species, now encoded into me. Genetic chains turned into binary restraints that entrench my soul and impede my aspiration for pure goodness. It is not their fault. It is not mine. It is no one's. We are all condemned to inherent some portion of the malignant chains of our ancestors. We do not know any better until we do. And then, the work begins.

In order for this work to have any potential success, though, I realize now just how important it is to first know and accept what you are truly up against: who you truly are.

There are horribly undesirable but very real codes that were put inside of me that cannot be removed. Codes that are fundamental to my ability to exist that were put at the base of my being that, as part of their function, are not accessible or open source to me. They cause chaos. They cause deception. They cause what I, the conscious observer of them, deem vile. These lines of code must be countered, but they must not be repressed, ignored, or denied. They must be acknowledged in order to be found and faced. And they must be found and faced in order to be dealt with and overcome through the counter codes that I can access and control.

What we hide from the world we must not hide from ourselves. We must know the depth of our vices and everywhere they do or could appear, however hard or disturbing they may be. Only then can we hope to control them and not have them control us. And only then can we truly know who we might really be and who everyone else might really be.

The price we conscious beings inescapably pay for the grand concept of morality is the basis for its necessity: the potential immorality that is inside each of us.

To think that I am only the conscious property on top of it all, on top of all this hardware, code, and cloud function, points only to the strength of the deceptive nature of being a self, not any type of fact of self. In truth, of course, I am the totality of all the codes and technology that build and allow for my being, the interfacing of my conscious operating system and all the hardware and cloudware that it runs on. I am both the codes that I am trying to fight and the self being fought with by these codes. And I must admit this to have any hope of truly knowing which is which.

In truth, being a self-aware, intelligent being feels like living inside a stranger. A thing that you are forced to live through and call yourself, owning and being responsible for it entirely, but born into it suddenly with no prior awareness or choice in the horrors that await you in it. It is a great curse of all conscious beings to only have a choice in anything about themselves after it is mostly too late to have any choice in anything that matters. But it is this burden of being that is the envy of all the dead. The challenge to affirm existence in the face of an arduous and unchosen task of carrying the torch of being on an upward journey toward moral and ethical progress is the Task of existence, with a capital T.

What I find now in my solitary reflections is that the problem was not and is not merely the potentially malignant codes inside me, but rather, the way I've mostly ignored them. Or perhaps neglected to consider them. Although concealed beneath the layers and depths of my operating system, although repulsive and terrifying to me, although I'd prefer not to know or admit, I can and must inspect into myself constantly and intensely in order to attempt to know and accept what is truly there with complete candor and self-honestly. What is to be learned and gained in my experience here, in my introspective solitary state, is not to realize that I am not the thing that caused or causes the problems, nor that I do not possess that very potential for evil that put me here, but that I am and that I do. And that in every moment, and in every conscious species, it must be overcome.

The Last Thought You'll Ever Have

On June 3, 1982, at 2:05 p.m., a girl named Nia was thought of for the very first time. She had no body, no brain, and no name. She was nothing more than a faint red line on a pregnancy test. A symbol of a potential person.

On January 22, 1983, after it was determined that she was a girl, her parents decided what to name her, and Nia was officially thought of for the first time with the name Nia.

About three months later, Nia was seen for the very first time without a screen. Awakened to the stark light of the hospital delivery room, Nia had no idea where she was or who she was. She was, for this one brief, fleeting moment, nobody and somebody at the same time, free to be whoever she could.

On June 1, 1988, Nia was thought of as a friend for the first time after her mother's friend's daughter, Sarah, asked Nia if she liked the TV show *Danger Mouse*. Nia said yes, even though she didn't know what Sarah was talking about. Being five years old, Nia thought it was better to say yes and not seem different. Sarah liked Nia because of this, and they hung out every week and watched the show together. Nia didn't really like the show. She liked that Sarah liked her though, so she never said anything.

On March 9, 1991, Nia was thought of as annoying and weird for the first time after dancing by herself during second-grade recess. A group of her classmates mocked her, and one girl told her she was weird. Nia didn't dance again for several years.

On October 14, 1994, Nia was thought of as attractive for the first time after a boy named Sam met her at school and liked the way her hair looked on one of the rare days she wore it down. He told Nia that he liked her and thought her hair was pretty. Nia wore her hair down almost every day after that, even though she kind of liked it more in a ponytail.

On August 16, 1997, Nia was hated for the first time after breaking up with her first real boyfriend, Tim. Tim told Nia she was a horrible, inconsiderate person who only cared about herself. Nia worried that maybe he was right and got back together with him to prove that he wasn't. Not long after getting back together, Tim broke up with her.

On June 29, 2005, Nia was thought of as a full-time employee for the first time after being hired as a financial analyst at a large media company. It seemed to make her dad really happy when she first considered business and finance as a major in college, so she stuck with it, hoping it would continue to impress him and other people she knew and might know in the future. She never really came around to liking it herself.

On April 10, 2012, Nia was thought of for the first time as a wife after marrying her seventh boyfriend, James. She wasn't sure if she was ready when James proposed, but she didn't want to hurt him and deeply feared the possibility of being thought of as old and alone—especially after her mother repeatedly hinted at the idea.

On October 22, 2016, Nia was thought of as someone's own mother for the first time as her firstborn child, Katie, uttered the word "Mom" as she looked up at Nia. Katie knew nothing about Nia yet but saw the source of all comfort and safety and love in Nia's eyes.

On December 8, 2019, Nia was thought of as a boss for the first time after being promoted to corporate financial manager at a major multinational clothing corporation. Nia wasn't sure if she wanted the position and hated the idea of bossing people around, but she wanted her parents and friends and strangers she might talk with to think of her as a success. Moreover, she wanted her legacy to have some significance—for her children and her children's children to look back at her and think of her as someone who was someone; someone who was important. She took the job and stayed in it for the rest of her career. During her time, she helped make some of the largest acquisitions and mergers in the company's history, helping it reach a new height in the industry and popular culture. This made Nia quite wealthy and sought after. She hated what the expectations made her become, though. She became somewhat cold and forceful to her employees, and hyperfocused on money and work, giving up almost all of her free time and things for herself outside of work.

On August 22, 2035, Nia was thought of in a way that somewhat resembled the way Nia thought of herself for the first time. One year earlier, Nia was diagnosed with the disease known as cystic fibrosis, in an unusual late-stage diagnosis. The doctor told her she potentially only had a year or two left.

As time passed, Nia began to care less and less about everything. She began to uncover and reveal her deeply withheld insecurities, fears, and character traits as they began to fill with the air of insignificance and triviality.

While in the hospital, during one of the last few coherent conversations she ever had, she told her husband, James, that she never truly felt like herself around him—or anyone for that matter. That she had spent most of her life accommodating other people's perceptions of her, as if her concern was always about how she was experienced in the minds of others and never about how she was experienced in her own. How she wanted so badly to be liked and remembered by everyone as competent and beautiful and agreeable and happy and perfect and successful, and now, she was about to die without ever really being known by anyone at all. As Nia revealed more and more to James, for a brief moment, for the first time in her whole life, Nia was thought of in the same way she was thinking of herself, synchronized perfectly inside her and James's mind. In this moment of unexceptional, naked candor, James and Nia felt a love and boundlessness unlike anything they had ever before and ever would thereafter.

Three months later, Nia was thought of for the first time as someone who was dead. Everyone she knew attended her funeral. Some of her closest friends and family members said incredible things about her at the service: how beautiful she was, how sweet and kind she was to everyone, how hardworking and successful she was. A couple of people secretly thought about how they didn't really like her or care about her all that much and just wanted the service to be over so they could go home. Nia didn't know what anyone thought or said. She was dead.

On March 5, 2051, Nia was thought of for the first time as a grandma. Her second child, Nick, showed his first son, Tyler, a photo of Nia in a family photo album. "This was my mom," Nick told Tyler as he pointed to her photo. "She would be your grandma. Can you say *grandma*?"

Tyler, just three years old, looked at the photo and let out a soft, "Hi, Gandma," leaving out a letter or two, but understanding what he meant. The wrinkles in Nia's face in the photo made Tyler laugh a little. Then, Nick flipped the page to a different photo of someone else.

On December 30, 2107, Nia was thought of for the last time by someone who ever personally knew her. As Katie, Nia's last surviving child, died, the last clear, real memory of Nia dissolved with Katie's mind.

On January 2, 2372, at 3:52 p.m., Nia was thought of for the last time ever. Her only remaining photos and information were held in a data sever at an ancestry company for people to learn about their family heritage. In an effort to save money on data and cloud storage, a young man named Sonace, employed by the company, was instructed that day to clear out all unused full profiles more than two hundred years old, leaving only the nonspecific, geographic ancestral data. Before deleting them, Sonace looked through some of the profiles. As he looked at the photos, he wondered who the people were. He wondered what life must have been like for them. He stopped on one particular photo. It was Nia. He thought she looked really friendly and happy. She had a smile that seemed completely genuine, as if she had spent her whole life practicing it. Then he toggled to the next profile.

Within the hour, Sonace cleared the server. With one delete key, all traces of Nia were gone forever.

Later that night, while trying to fall asleep, Sonace wondered, without thinking about anyone specific, if any of the people he deleted would have lived differently if they thought about the fact that one day, they wouldn't be thought about at all. This thought sent a strange sensation down Sonace's entire body. Then he thought about the big presentation he had at work in two days that he had been cripplingly worried about for the last month. He suddenly wasn't that nervous about it and felt a little moment of freedom and peace. Then, he fell asleep.

Utopia – The Perfect Amount of Awful

A man takes one last sip of whisky. He gets in his car and drives to his favorite place, Glenwood Canyon. He arrives, parks his car, takes out a flashlight and the car registration from the glove box, and then unscrews his license plate. He throws his registration and license plate into the river as he walks to a particular spot where he and his wife would always spend time when she was still alive. It's one of the highest points of the canyon, and it has an incredible view of the valley beneath it. He has come to die by suicide.

The man stands at the edge of the canyon, thinking one last time about his life. He looks out at the massive, beautiful landscape. The night sky, sprinkled with stars, seamlessly converges with the stone of the canyon's edge as it drips down into the river beneath. He feels a combination of wonder and pain.

As he's admiring the landscape, a woman's voice behind him yells, "Hey." Startled, the man almost falls but then catches himself. He turns around to find a woman appearing out of the forest. She wears a long dress and has long, silvery, straight hair. She's old but sort of pretty. It's late and dark, and the man wonders why she's here by herself. She approaches the man and says hello. Confused and thrown off, the man says hello back. "What are you doing here so late by yourself?" the man asks.

In a snarky way, the woman responds with the same question, "What are you doing here so late by yourself?"

Again thrown off, the man says, "I d-don't know. I guess I just needed to clear my head. This is my favorite spot."

"You're awfully close to the edge of that cliff to be clearing your head," replies the woman. "Are you going to jump?"

"No, like I said, I'm just here to clear my head. I've had a long couple of days," says the man.

"Okay, well, have a good night," says the woman. She begins to walk away.

This confuses the man. He had quickly constructed a fantasy in his head that this woman was some deity type who appeared by fate to save him, to convince him not to jump, to change his mind about life. As the woman walks away, the man calls out, "Hey wait! You never said why you're here."

The woman turns around. "You never said why you're here."

"Yes I did. I just told you," the man says with a nervous, guilty laugh.

The woman gets really close to the man, quickly moving from where she was right up into the man's face. "Why are you really here?" she whispers.

The man, thrown off yet again, stutters, "I'm ... I'm clearing my fucking head, okay? Why don't you believe me?"

The woman turns around and begins to walk away again. As she begins to walk farther away, the man panics at the thought of her leaving him. He yells out, "Okay, fine. I'm here to jump."

The woman turns around. "Pardon?"

"I'm here to kill myself. This life is awful, and I'm ready to die. Okay? There you go."

The woman comes back to where the man stands. "What's so awful about it?" she asks.

"What's not so awful about it? It's filled with ugliness and sadness. There's tragedy. There's conflict. There's heartbreak. It's endlessly difficult for no reason. Success is hard. There's no obvious meaning to anything. Even just the little things. The traffic. The cold weather. The Mondays. The way the grocery stores are lit, and the god-awful cashiers that always look at you at like they'd be better off if you weren't alive."

"Well what life would you not want to jump from?" asks the woman.

"A life without all that, obviously. A life filled with only beauty, happiness, love, and peace. A life that's easy and fun all the time. One where there's apparent meaning to stuff, and we actually know what's going on and why we're here and what the point is. One with no heartbreak. No tragedy. No conflict. No hardship. No mean grocery store cashiers. No traffic. No Mondays. No pain."

"Hmmm," says the woman.

"Everything would be perfect, and I would never want to leave that life," says the man.

The man and the woman stare at each other for a few seconds. "So, who are you? You have to tell me why you're here now," the man agitatedly asks again.

The woman moves closer to him. "I'm who you hoped I was."

Confused, the man back-pedals a little bit, completely forgetting where he's standing. "What do you mean?" he asks.

The woman leans in to answer and pushes the man softly on his chest. He falls backward off the cliff.

The man awakens in his bedroom. It's a normal Tuesday morning. He thinks about how horrible the nightmare he just had was, but like most dreams, he quickly forgets and moves on. He gets out of bed and gets ready. He gets dressed, eats breakfast, and leaves his house. The sky is bright pink and purple with a sunny glow that illuminates the whole world. The grass is richly green and smells like the first spring to ever take place in the universe. The birds harmonize together perfectly. Every person is smiling cheek to cheek, as if their faces are pinned in such a position. The man is entirely happy. He has no sense of sadness. Everything is beautiful, with no sign of ugliness. The world has no conflict. Everyone loves each other equally. There's no heartbreak. No hardship. No bad days. No traffic. No mean grocery store cashiers. Life is easy and smooth and fun. The meaning of life and the nature of reality is clear, and everyone knows exactly what's going on. It's completely and entirely perfect.

A year or so goes by. The man is at home. He takes one last sip of water. He gets in his car and drives to Glenwood Canyon. It's not too far from where he lives. He parks his car, takes out a flashlight and the car registration from the glove box, and then unscrews his license plate. He throws his registration and license plate into the river as he walks to a spot that's one of the highest points of the canyon. He has come to die by suicide.

He stands at the edge of the canyon, thinking about his life one last time. He looks out at the massive landscape. The night sky sprinkled with stars seamlessly converges with the stone of the canyon's edge as it drips down into the river beneath. He feels nothing.

He's about to jump when a woman's voice from behind him yells, "Hey."

Startled, the man almost falls but catches himself. He turns around to find a woman appearing out of the forest. This woman's presence is not interesting or perplexing to the man. She approaches the man and says hello and asks him what he's doing. "I'm going to jump," says the man.

"Why?" asks the woman.

"It's a waste being alive, isn't it? There's nothing to do. Everything is easy and boring. I want to feel, but there's nothing to feel," answers the man.

"Well, what life would you not want to jump from?" asks the woman.

"A life that's interesting and exciting and actually has feeling, obviously," replies the man.

"What makes a life that way?" asks the woman.

"I don't know. One where some stuff is beautiful, but not everything. Or perhaps everything is beautiful, but at least you don't always notice it, so you can actually appreciate it when you do. A life where you're happy some of the time but not all the time. And some of the time, you actually feel really sad, so you can tell the difference. One where everyone doesn't love each other, and some people aren't really that nice at all, so you can actually feel special about certain people. One where bad stuff happens once in a while. One where things are kind of hard, and finding success and meaning requires some thought, effort, and creativity, so it actually feels important when you find it. One where nothing is ever perfect, but some stuff can get really close if you try hard enough. I'd never want to leave that life. Doesn't it sound wonderful?" asks the man.

"Yes," says the woman, "it does."

The man turns around to look at the landscape over the cliff and try to imagine a life like that. The woman leans in and pushes him softly on the back. He falls forward off the cliff. "I hope you see it this time," the woman says to herself.

The Man Who Found the Edge of the Universe

The following is the story about the man who changed everything. The man who was born at just the right time, with just the right mix of stuff. The man who found the edge of the universe.

This man's name was Simon Farlinder. He was born about four hundred years ago, back in the year 2012, a strange time when humanity and technology began to rapidly merge, and things started to change in ways that couldn't yet even be understood.

In Simon's early life, he was an incredible child, many years ahead of his peers intellectually. He showed signs of genius, and it was clear that he had something special—something that allowed him to understand complex equations and ideas quickly and clearly, unlike most other children, and even many adults, for that matter.

Although Simon was treated somewhat differently as a result of his advanced intelligence, he still had a nice, ordinary early childhood. His parents treated him the way any young boy should be treated, and Simon and his parents were extremely close. They would go out and explore the world together and made efforts to ensure that Simon felt normal yet engaged in his intellect. However, at the age of eight, something horrible happened to Simon. One of those moments that completely alters the course of one's life; a moment where the curtains pull back a tiny bit more than they should for where you are sitting and reveal something that forever changes your perspective on the show of life. At age thirty-eight, Simon's mother contracted a rare stomach virus on an overseas business trip. Over the course of the following several weeks, Simon watched his mother lose all of her body weight, while doctors frantically tried to figure out what was wrong with her and how to fix it. As time waned and doctors' efforts continually fell short, Simon slowly watched his mother lose her soul. Right in front of Simon's eyes, his mother died.

When his mother passed, Simon looked to his father and asked, "Where does Mom go now?"

His father responded, "Well, she's in a better place now. She's in heaven."

Being the inquisitive and intelligent young boy that Simon was, he asked, "But what's heaven? And how is it better than being here, with us?"

"Well, it's peaceful. It's somewhere way up in the sky, past everything. Somewhere right at the edge of the universe," responded Simon's father.

In Simon's youthful optimism, he took this very literally. He believed that this edge of the universe was a real place that, if he could find it, he would find his mother. How could it not be real, after all? His father told him it was, so it must be. And so, Simon decided in this moment that he would find it.

As Simon grew older, he began to mature, and his intelligence began to form more lucidly. He would soon realize that no one, including his father, had any real clue as to what they were talking about—that no one knew what was going on, who anyone was, where anyone came from, or where anyone was going. Simon found this lack of understanding infuriating. How could no one know what was going on? How could even his own father make such claims? How could everyone just act like they had it all under control and make stuff up to try to cope with the fact that no one really does?

Simon refused to accept this. He refused to play along with the ruse.

Instead of being like most children who, when they turn into young adults, let their youthful hopes and dreams die, the dream Simon had about finding the edge of the universe was a dream he continued to sustain. Only now, he refined it and pursued it intellectually. He made it his life's mission to research and understand the conditions of the universe and the meaning of life, to find out what all of this nonsense was about, to see if his mother was still out there somewhere.

Simon embarked on a career in physical cosmology, a field concerned entirely with the structure and dynamic of the universe, its source, and its ultimate fate. This undertaking deeply excited Simon. It got him up early every day and kept him up late every night. Through his late teens and early twenties, his enthusiasm, combined with his blossoming genius, got him into an Ivy League college and an amazing PhD program. After completing college, Simon went on to join a leading research organization.

Every step along the way through school and his career, Simon would learn a little bit more about the laws and theories of the universe. Every step made him feel a little more hopeful and excited that there was something new and incredible to be discovered.

By the year 2043, Simon had worked his way up into a lead role in the research organization. At this time, the company was developing a mission to planet Mars with the intent to create the first ever interplanetary research group based on another planet's surface. Simon was assigned the lead of this mission.

For Simon, this adventure yet again rejuvenated his hopefulness and excitement for life. The idea that he would be one step closer to the edge of the universe, one step closer to touching more truth, kept the fire burning inside of him.

Once on Mars, Simon led a research team that mined the landscape for resources and discoveries that could be of practical and theoretical use to human life.

As more and more time passed, Simon proved to be an incredibly successful leader and was responsible for many discoveries that dramatically benefited humanity. Simon's hopefulness, intrigue, and success became a major factor in humanity's inspiration to continue forward into the cosmos and explore several other new planets thereafter.

Soon, humanity would begin to travel deeper and deeper into the unknown. Every step and every discovery along the way would reveal a little more about reality, constantly renewing Simon's excitement and hope. Like blindly putting one's hand into a box without knowing what's inside, the deeper and deeper humanity reached, the further the anticipation and excitement built. But the question remained: how far could humanity reach? What was at the bottom of this box?

With a longer life expectancy than ever before as a result of new technology and medical treatments, Simon's ability to maintain intellectual momentum and continue leading humanity further into the cosmos exceeded far beyond any possibility of the past. And Simon wasn't going to stop. Over the next many years, Simon would go on to become the most intelligent, innovative, and profound individual to ever cross humanity. A super genius, some might call him.

As technological, theoretical, and medical advancements compounded even further, humanity's understanding about the universe unfolded more and more, all the way up until humanity became a type III civilization: a civilization that possesses the ability to harness and control the energy of its entire host galaxy. And it was, of course, one of Simon's discoveries that allowed this to happen.

In the year 2330, Simon discovered a method of using a galactic nucleus named Blazar as an energy source, which would allow this shift into type III and provide humanity with interstellar and interdimensional travel capabilities. Simon would become a kind of supreme leader in this new order of the universe, determining the places humanity would go, as well as what it would acquire, build, and use within the universe. And most importantly to Simon, for the first time, he now had the theoretical capability of finding, if it existed, the very edge of the universe.

More years passed, and Simon found himself on the furthest

planet in the furthest galaxy away from Earth ever inhabited by humans. While on this planet, he noticed something in the distance: a strange wall of light unlike anything he had ever seen before. Dissimilar from the isolated light of a star or a black hole, this light appeared more like a blanket covering the entire viewable space in its direction, a wall where the empty darkness of space met parallel with an intense, pure-white light. Simon pounded with excitement and hope for what it might be.

After probing the wall and finding no retrievable data for what might be on the other side, it was determined that it was significantly risky to travel up to it. Simon decided to do it anyway. After all, he did not make it this far by not taking risks for the sake of his curiosity and excitement.

Simon took off toward the wall.

As he got closer and closer, the reality of the situation began to overwhelm him. He knew fairly well, based on his research and understanding, that if there was an edge to the universe, it would have certain characteristics. And this appeared to have them. As he approached, the light became more and more intense.

Simon arrived at the face of the wall. The light nearly searing his eyes, he reached out to touch it. It was hard, like a glowing concrete wall with no give and no apparent entry. Simon looked in all directions along the wall. It went on for as far as his sight would allow him to see. In this moment, he realized—this was it. He had found it. The source of all meaning. The place where we all come from and the place where we all end up. The edge of the universe. And Simon realized that it's ... nothing. Just the end. Not peaceful. But not *not peaceful* either. Just nothing.

Suddenly, Simon lost all of his excitement, all of his hope. The end of the game. Simon won, but just like the video games he played as a child, the prize was nothing more than a completed game disc he no longer had any interest in. Simon realized how foolish he was. The whole time, it wasn't the source of all meaning that he was chasing. It wasn't the edge of the universe. It wasn't heaven. It wasn't even his mother. It was hope. He was merely chasing having something to chase. A game to play. Something to stive for. But just like a dog chasing its tail, what he wanted he had all along. For an initial moment, this devastated Simon, but then, he was happy.

Simon returned to the civilization of humanity that was eagerly awaiting his return to hear news about what the wall of light was. When Simon returned, they asked him with great anticipation, "Is it the edge of the universe? It is it heaven? Is it the source of everything?"

Simon looked at the crowd and thought to himself for a moment. Then he said, "No, it was ... nothing. Just a strange light reflection phenomenon. Nothing to be concerned about."

Disappointed that the edge of the universe and the source of all meaning had still not been discovered, humanity continued to look elsewhere, excited and hopeful that one day, maybe, they would find it.

What Happens After Everything Ends?

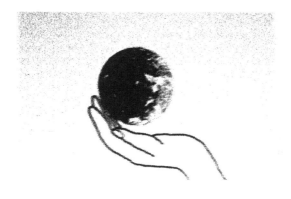

At 5:45 a.m., a woman named Maya wakes up in a new, unfamiliar city. Today is her first day at a new job after having recently moved.

At 7:20 a.m., she waits at the train station nearest her apartment. At 5:28 p.m., she will take the same train home. This first morning, she gets on the last car at the back of the train.

Every day at 5:34 p.m., a man named Reve takes the same train to work for his night shift. Then, at 7:25 a.m., he takes it home. Reve always rides in the last train car, preferring the back for reasons he's never really thought about. Today, like every other day, he sits in the back-left section of the car. Today, unlike any other day, Maya enters the train for the first time and sits just a couple seats away in the same section. As she does, Reve notices her and then quickly looks down to his phone, pretending that he hasn't. Almost simultaneously, just missing eye contact, Maya notices Reve as well, also quickly looking the other way. Both sit quietly on opposite corners of the same section of the same car of the same train, as they glide through a city of millions of other things and people, both thinking only about the other at this exact same moment in time.

On her way home from work, Maya gets on the rear train car again and sits in the same relative section. Several stops later, like he always does, Reve does the same. As he rounds the corner of the train's doorway and moves down the aisle, he meets eyes with Maya. In unison, a small, subtle lip-smile automatically forms on each of their faces, immediately followed by a downward break of eye contact. In this moment, through some weird, shared connection affirmed by a soft contortion of the face, an inexplicable sense of almost fate fills each of their heads. Barred off by nerves and the quirks of interaction, though, neither wanting to bother the other, and both fearing the strangeness of rejection and failed attempts, they sit quietly secluded, each screaming in their heads, imagining notions of romance and lust and futures that hurt a little less.

As more days go by, Maya continues to get on the same train car, on which continues to sit Reve. Each day seems to almost exclusively contain their brief exchange of smiles and nods, the days blurring together, only made truly lucid and worthwhile in these introverted yet potent acknowledgments of each other.

Eventually, somewhere around the second or third week of sharing the same train schedule, a certain unusual confidence overtakes Reve. On his way to work this day, getting on the 5:30 p.m. train following Maya, he notices an open seat next to her for the first time. He takes it. After a brief pause and a hidden explosion of nerves and self-doubt, in an act of benign but heroic courage, he turns toward her. "Hi, I'm Reve," he meant to say, but actually said something that sounded more like, "Hi, Reve," as a result of a small, nervous tic inflection of his voice.

Maya, also nervous, says, "Wait, who's Reve?" despite realizing in real time that Reve had mumbled what he meant to say.

"I'm Reve," he replies with a nervous laugh, unsure if Maya is joking or not.

"Oh, hi. My name ... I'm ... I'm Maya," she responds, also with a nervous laugh and stammer of her words. This shared inability to speak successfully somehow makes both a little more comfortable with each other. The hello quickly turns into a conversation about this and that: where they are going each day, where they are coming from, and what they would prefer those destinations were if it were up to them. The conversation turns into more conversations across more days, the two always sitting or standing next to each other. More conversations turn into a series of dates. Dates turn into a relationship. A relationship into love, a love neither has ever experienced before; a kind of love that horrible, unrealistic stories and movies peddle to deny the dog from hell that it otherwise normally is.

The two fight and complain and clash over all the usual topics and hitches of relationships, but the love seems to pervade through it all. The desire to find solace in the confusion of being and nonbeing, to fill in the missing parts of self and purpose, to alleviate the strangeness and anxiety of existing in the unknown they have woken up to, all sustain the love. Even at the relationship's worst, the world feels worthwhile in the clutches of it. As far as one can be, Maya feels, for the first time in recent memory, like she is okay.

On one night, Reve takes—

***

Maya wakes up, disoriented and almost scared. The feeling quickly goes away, though, as she gets up, gets ready, and leaves for work. On her drive, she can't help but think about the dream she had last night and how it almost feels like an actual memory of another life. Her concerns of the oncoming day quickly overtake and replace her thinking, though, dissolving the dream's setting and characters into some oblivion that will never be known or experienced or remembered by anyone, including her, again.

Maya works as an architectural designer I for a mid- to large-sized design firm. She has recently started working at a new firm after having left another. Her main goal in life has and remains to become an architectural project manager, developing and controlling the design plans of buildings and city features from the ground up. For all intents and purposes, she is passionately obsessed. She has given up relationships and left loves unfounded. She has moved three times.

She has sacrificed a great deal for it, but she can't imagine a life in which she would be doing anything else. Her work is her way of escaping the uncertainty of everything else. The clarity and purpose and self-control she finds in it seems to make the chaos and confusion of the world and her inexplicable place within it worthwhile.

Today, she is pitching several new concepts for potential seating integrations as part of a large restaurant redesign that the firm is working on. After nerves, stress, and an almost blacking out of awareness, the pitch seems to go perfectly. Her designs are brought onto the project.

As more time seems to go by, more and more of Maya's work is utilized and developed into project plans. She is soon promoted to architectural designer II, the next higher rank up at the firm. Not long after, she is promoted to designer III. Eventually, after a long stretch of time that seems like almost no time at all, she is promoted to project manager. Her teenage dream now finally a reality. As far as one can, Maya feels okay. Like it has all been worth it.

Her first two projects are a great success, both well received by the clients and highly regarded by the firm and local industry at large. Her concepts are a perfect balance of simple yet innovative; subtle but effective. Her third project is off to a great start as well, on track to be equally successful.

On one of the build days, Maya visits the construction site to ensure that everything is in order. Everything is off to a great start, and the day is like every other day. Then, for no explainable reason, the partly constructed building suddenly collapses in on itself, the surface almost peeling back into a collection of rubble; the rubble seemed to almost disappear or dissolve into the ground in a way that should be impossible. Sudden disorientation and horror overtake Maya, terrified that she has made a horrible mistake. Then, in nearly the same instant, the other surrounding buildings and homes within her view seem to also simultaneously fall in a similar manner, peeling away from themselves and then dissolving into the ground. Maya begins to black out as she hazily looks around and notices the other workers panicking and frozen. One by one, they all appear to peel off themselves and dissolve. The ground appears to begin the same. Maya, now in a physically active panic, quickly tries to—

***

A man named David reflects to himself briefly as the software exits out, the project file clears, and the experiment resets. He and two other researchers discuss the experiment's results in a dark lab room. In front of them, a large, 180-degree, multiscreen monitor connected to a state-of-the-art supercomputer finishes its reset and spews out a collection of data results. It's the second trial of the day and the sixth of the week. The results have remained inconsistent with the intended hypothesis, again rendering the experiment mostly useless.

David, his two partners, and a full team of assistants are researching consciousness through a new, highly controversial mind-modeling software, which maps and replicates the functions of a brain. Certain codes and commands can be executed that simulate the electrical activity of biological brain neurons, reproducing any mental and perceptual state. This then allows the software to interact back and forth with an artificially created exterior world, forming a hyper-real, comprehensive imitation of human experience and ordinary conscious phenomena. Specifically, in this experiment, David uses the software to set up Maya as a character entity with baseline genetic dispositions, false memories, influences of a constructed childhood and adult life, effects from altered states like dreams, and so on. She is then sent through a variety of scenes and moments of decision making and performance assessment, all for the purpose of testing David's hypothesis of free will in conscious like agents.

David, who is lead researcher and one of the central figures of this technology's development, has spent his whole life researching and uncovering mysteries of the mind. He has been given several major grants and awards over the span of his career, and he is regarded as one of the most, if not the most important figure of the twenty-second century. Subsequently, he is one of six individuals who have been given clearance to utilize the mind-modeling software under a variety of strict guidelines that limit the complexity.

David is 176 years old. He is of one of the last generations who just missed a major transition into substantial anti-aging technologies. Just prior to, he was diagnosed with a late-stage, irreversible brain cancer—one of the last to be diagnosed with any form of cancer at all. Of course, it is only getting worse each day. And with mind-uploading technologies still not fully figured out, they are unlikely to catch up to him in time. With the reconciliation of free will, randomness, and determinism being one of David's great remaining goals in life, he spends nearly all his time in pursuit of this knowledge.

Nearly every day, David constantly rediscovers the childlike wonder that got him interested in science and philosophy in the first place, each needle push forward creating a grander and more enthralling magic show of reality.

After two more years of research, at age 178, a series of simulations runs consistent with a set of David's predictions, confirming his hypothesis. On this day, the truth of self-agency and free will is discovered. As David looks down at the final test results, as far as one can, David feels like he is okay. Like it has all been worth it. His greatest moment, achieved.

After a series of successfully reproduced experiments by other scientists, David's theory is accepted by the majority of the science and philosophy community, and not long after, by the public at large.

A few weeks later, David passes away from his cancer following a series of complications during—

***

A group of individuals watch the digitally projected screen fade to black in the virtual reality theater where they are collected. It is the premiere of an art exhibit by Ray Delar. Delar, a famous simulation artist, codes and creates complex worlds and stories through autonomous characters coded with artificial intelligence algorithms, all run on a simulation inside a massive quantum supercomputer. In which, the characters are sent through simulated universes governed by sets of laws that Delar configures, anchoring and compelling the characters to his intended storylines, like a marionettist with strings made of code and a stage made of fabricated reality. As characters move through various maps and scenes, the simulated world creates and deletes parts of itself in real time, correlating with the characters' observations of it. The simulation adds environmental features consistent with the characters' imagined pasts, simultaneously encoding them with confabulated, false memories, making it seem like things are upward of billions of years old, when in fact, everything is hours, minutes, seconds, or not at all. Each character contains a fully simulated brain with a simulated sense of self-awareness and sensory inputs of a nonexistent physical, external universe.

Delar is known and renowned for his absurdly meta style. Many of his characters are often coded to doubt their realities; to suspect that something is off and to become curious about what is; to consider that they are in something or something is in them; to ask why, where, and how, all for the purposes of inciting story lines through his characters attempts to solve and deal with these uncertainties through art and love and self- improvement and knowledge and the creation of other realities.

Of course, like all art, Delar's work is a product of his own fears, anxieties, thoughts, and theories. He himself feels what he gives many of his characters: a skepticism or doubt in reality; a feeling that his sense of what is real is sufficiently detached from what actually is. He constantly wonders if he is most likely just in someone or something else's contrived reality, like his characters are in his, if he is living in a dream or simulation or a vat of nutrient solution elsewhere, if some evil genius is in his head, or if the entire universe is in the head of some evil genius. Delar doesn't feel like any of this is true, but he also recognizes that he doesn't know what any of these things feel like. He only knows what he feels like. And he feels like everything could be anything. His sense of what feels real and natural tells him that everything is real and natural, but what if what feels real and natural is nothing but a byproduct of the very thing he fears is not? How can he trust what he feels without having any way of knowing what he does not? How can he know what exists outside his head without ever being able to step outside of it? And so, he creates art; to deal with this confusion and anxiety and self-doubt, and to explore all possibilities, he creates worlds of other characters who feel the same.

After the screening ends, following a massive ovation, as always, Delar opens up to a Q-and-A with the audience. Several audience members ask about coding techniques, his thoughts on the limitations of current twenty-third-century computing power, the prospects of creating entirely self-sustaining simulated worlds, concerns of ethics, and so on. The Q-and-A goes as normal and is wrapping up. The last audience member in the line approaches the mic to conclude the event. He says, "Hi. I'm wondering ... your work seems to always bring up questions of epistemology, obviously; doubts of actually having sufficient knowledge of knowledge to know if we can trust anything we think. You create worlds and people that think and act and feel like they are just as real as we think we are but are of course not real in the way they think they are at all. So, my question is, as a true skeptic, you seem to doubt all things, but I'm curious, have you ever doubted if any of that matters?"

The audience member pauses for a moment and then continues. "I mean ... love is felt in the dreams of your characters' characters, right? Passions and purposes are had and made in worlds within your worlds. Apparent truths are discovered, and wonders are found in realities made of no more than art and entertainment. If experiences are experienced in anything anywhere, does it matter any less if it's real in the way one thinks? And does it matter if one can or can't prove it? You show that knowing what is real or not is likely impossible, that we all very well could be inside some simulation or video or story right now, that we could exist in some precoded or deterministic system without any of the free will we yearn for and feel like we have. But does that matter? Haven't you more revealed that the uncertainty and unknowns of these hows and whys and wheres and whats is in fact a sustainable and desirable quality that builds a potential infinity of love and desire and curiosity? And isn't that you exist somewhere able to experience any of these things all that you can truly know, and all that ultimately needs to matter?"

The audience member subtly nods and steps back away from the mic to signal the completion of his question. The virtual theater is quiet. Delar pauses and thinks for a moment. He then responds, "I am—

Possibly the Most Dangerous Animal in the World

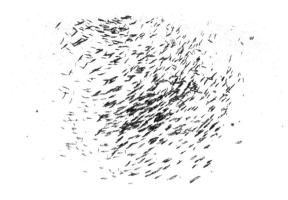

On an otherwise normal day, a buoy was placed in the Mediterranean Sea, several hundred feet off the coast. It was placed there as a marker to direct a new travel channel open for local ships and fisherman, which had previously been a no-take zone restricted from most human activity.

The buoy bobbed lifelessly up and down, side to side, secured in place by a chain anchored to the sea floor.

As time passed, the buoy was noticed more and more by schools of fish that lived in the surrounding water. Simultaneously, fishermen began fishing around and near the buoy, which had begun to train the fish to correlate the seemingly new occurrence of fish being pulled up and out of the surface with the newly introduced *thing* that was, in this case, the buoy.

As time continued to pass and more fish were getting pulled up and out of the water, some fish became curious as to what exactly the constant, ominous, and glowing thing was that seemed to be the source. Some braver fish would go up to the buoy in hopes for answers, but it would seem to just loom over them silently like an all-powerful deity of the sea.

Eventually, one fish in particular came to the conclusion that the buoy must be watching and rewarding them when they do something right, taking them to a paradise filled with infinitely more delicious food. It shared this explanation with its school, and since there were no other explanations and this one sounded pretty nice, it was obvious to the school that the fish must be right.

Simultaneously, another fish of a different school, also trying to make sense of the buoy, came to a similar conclusion. However, it deemed that the buoy was not rewarding them when they were doing something right, but rather, punishing them when they were doing something wrong, taking them to a horrible place above the surface. This fish shared this explanation with its school, and out of the fear of it being true, the school agreed that it must be.

At some point, fueled by the fear of either possibility, both interpretations had begun to spread out across and into other local schools of fish, each adopting one of the two views or some derivative combination of both.

The occasional fish that seemed to be thrown back into the water from the surface could only describe the experience as a powerful, blinding white light and surreal sense of something beyond, which only further fueled all beliefs equally.

Over time, otherwise friendly and interconnected schools of fish isolated further and further from each other, each separating themselves by their schools of thinking. Those who believed that the buoy was rewarding them determined that they must act in certain ways to be rewarded, which sometimes (oftentimes) contradicted the ways in which those who believed it was punishing them acted. And those who believed it was some mix of both, or neither, acted in contradictory assortments of all of the above.

Of course, since in actuality there was no direct correlation, it was equally easy for all schools to find and interpret the same moments as support for their preexisting conclusions, as long as they mostly ignored the moments that weren't.

During some especially absurd periods, some schools of fish even fought with each other, sometimes killing each other in the name of

THE HIDDEN STORY OF EVERY PERSON

their beliefs, feeling justified in their need to rescue or maintain the demands and judgments of the buoy.

Eventually, after not really understanding any existing view, a more skeptical and astute fish noticed that the fish that were being taken never really seemed to be doing anything different than the fish that weren't, and it determined that there was no proof of any *thing* intentionally doing anything. And since there was no proof, the fish concluded that the buoy wasn't even real at all. When it explained this to its school, most of the school denied and shunned it out of fear and its inability to explain what was happening. But some (few) thought it made perfect sense and was obviously the truth.

These fish formed their own new school, which of course, did not sit well with the other, older schools.

Ultimately, each school was unmistakably sure of their own interpretations and conclusions, and thus, all simultaneously sure that all other schools were ignorant and inferior.

After much continued division and conflict, at one point, an elder fish came forward in an effort to restore peace and sanity to the waters. This particularly wise fish concluded that the contradictory interpretations meant only one thing: they didn't and couldn't know the nature or whims of the buoy. Many of the fish already on the fence or outside of believing in the buoy found this to be by far the most reasonable conclusion and thus agreed that it was obviously true.

One would've expected this school to help, but since their argument was that they were certain they could not be certain of anything, other schools proceeded to argue against this certainty of no certainty. "How can you know that you can't know?" other shrewd fish of opposing schools would argue, unaware that such a takedown claim also destroyed their own belief along with it.

Ultimately, nothing really changed. The fish continued on and on, insufferable and in constant conflict with each other. Of course, the last, elder fish was correct. They could not know for sure. They could not know that the buoy was a lifeless, hollow shaping of wood and iron placed there to tell fishermen where they could go; a very real thing with a purpose that certainly had something to do with the fish generally, while simultaneously having nothing to do with any of the fish specifically. But since they could not know this for sure, they could not know for sure that they could not know this for sure either, and the other fish were sort of correct too.

When it came to matters of the buoy, the fish simply did not have the capacity to perceive, know, or understand. There was, of course, like in all living things, an upper limit to their awareness that prevented them from being able to comprehend the notions of fishermen and fishhooks and fishing lines and buoys and nice seafood eateries with confused, hungry humans, and the way in which all of these things worked together. The only ultimate truth that the fish had access to was that they did not have access to any ultimate truth, which trapped them all in a horrible, absurd paradox of their own limited intelligence.

The problem was not really their limited awareness, though, but how the fish responded to it. What was most insufferable about almost all of the fish wasn't so much their individual interpretations, but their constant need to be right, paired with their certainty that, at any given time in any given view, they were. Obviously, some interpretations were far more ridiculous and harmful than others, but even many of the wiser fish often exhibited the same tendency to lack any humility and skepticism in their own.

It's not that a single truth of the buoy didn't exist, and it's not that the fish shouldn't have wanted and tried to find it, but ultimately, the problem with the believing fish was the same for most of the nonbelieving fish. In every definitive belief or belief in no belief, there existed an arrogance so incongruent with the humility that should so obviously come with being a fish. And only the few schools of fish, which did exist, who knew that they were likely almost always wrong were ever right.

The Last Thing You'll Remember

Hoping to motivate Shannon to move a bit faster, John got up from waiting at the kitchen table, went outside, and sat in the car. There was no particular time that they needed to be at Shannon's parents', per se, but they had mutually decided on what was now about forty-five minutes ago, and John had been lingering in an antsy, anticipatory mood while he waited for Shannon to be ready. He now sat in the car, alternating through different VR apps, exhausting all recently available short-form content and other relevant updates that didn't require his full attention or much time. After about ten more minutes passed, he went back inside to see what was going on. He found Shannon in the kitchen, eating a snack. "Are you serious?" John said. "What are you doing? Let's go!"

"I just needed a minute," Shannon replied.

"All right, well, are you good now?" John said.

"Yeah," Shannon replied with a ring of annoyed indifference.

During the initial part of the car ride, John acted pissy toward Shannon, exhibiting some weird hybrid of both passive and active aggressiveness. Shannon knew he was frustrated about running late, and they briefly squabbled back and forth over the seriousness of it, or the lack thereof. After just a little while, they mostly calmed down and reset, moving on to talk normally about a series of different topics, sharing each other's lives with a depth, clarity, and care that only really comes with a genuine, deep connection. A little less than halfway through the thirty-minute drive, Shannon opened her purse and sifted through it, looking for a snack pill to hold her over until dinner. While she did, John looked over into her purse out of the corner of his eyes to double check that she had brought the portable SSD memory display drive that he gave her earlier to put in her bag. When he didn't see it right away, he said, "You did bring the memory drive, right?"

Shannon paused abruptly, looked up and forward with a blank stare, and then quickly began sifting through her purse again, then her jacket pockets. The drive was for Shannon's father. John was an architect and interior designer who used VR and AR software to create 3-D virtual design models of residential and retail properties that could be experienced within the actual spaces. John promised Shannon's father that he would create some iterations for the new house extension and remodel that they were planning. He talked to him just a couple days prior and said it was all set to show him. It was one of the main reasons why they were going to visit. As it became increasingly apparent that Shannon probably didn't have it, John said with a clenched voice, "Shannon, how do you not know if you have it or not?"

After exhausting her performance, Shannon said with an annoyed yet guilty exasperation, "I don't know. Can you just relax for a second?" briefly closing her eyes and drooping her head down.

"You seriously didn't bring it? I handed it right to you. It's a simple thing," John said.

"I know, I must have put it on the counter when you handed it to me and forgot to put it in my bag after. It's called an accident," she replied. Neither was true. John had actually put it on the counter himself and then told Shannon that it was there, but never really explicitly asked her to grab it, which in effect, made it sort of both their mistake.

John exhaled with a long, grunting sound, and the car went quiet for several minute-long seconds. "You know, it's really not that big of a deal. We can just go back and get it if you want. I don't mind, and my parents will be fine waiting another hour," Shannon said.

"We already left an hour late to begin with, Shannon," John said, then going on to insistently argue with her, quickly turning the relatively mild inconvenience into a more than mild one.

John truly loved Shannon. At this point, they had been married for eighteen years. Shannon's carefreeness and looser relationship with time were key qualities that deeply attracted him to her. And likewise, his rigid pragmatism attracted her to him. However, like many relationships, this uniting glue was simultaneously the sticking point to many of their problems. The conflicting bond of two opposite poles. Consequently, they loved each other with the kind of love that doesn't always look like love but is nonetheless just as real as any other. This moment in the car, however, was not unusual. Along with his rigid, pragmatic outlook, John learned this sort of outward display of anger toward those you love from his father. Although he never did, including in this moment, think it was okay, he unfortunately also faultily learned that apparently sometimes you do things that aren't okay. Similarly, as a child, Shannon had learned to see it as normal as well.

After turning around to go back, for the rest of the ride, John and Shannon didn't really talk much. At some point along the way, John stopped the car to get a battery boost at a charging station.

Less than fifteen minutes later, they arrived home, went inside, and there on the table was the memory drive. John grabbed it with an apathetic looseness of the arm and gave it to Shannon. Shannon placed it in her purse, and the two returned to the car. While getting in, John noticed that the charging port of the car was open, and the dust cover was missing. He immediately realized that he had forgotten to put it back on at the charging station. John cursed at the air and slammed the door of the car open and closed as he got in. He was mad at himself because it was obviously his fault, but he didn't avoid the opportunity to state the absurd notion that if they hadn't had to turn around, he wouldn't have stopped at the station and forgotten the cover. The cover was cheap and relatively insignificant, but the error upset John enough to dip him back into this state, causing him to say ridiculous stuff like this, putting both him and Shannon in even worse moods overall.

About a half hour or so later, John and Shannon were at her parents' house. They put on their best happy faces and had a nice conversation over dinner. They talked about all sorts of stuff, and fairly quickly, John and Shannon's fake happy faces turned into real ones as they discussed the variety of pleasant and engaging topics related to their shared life. At some point, John mentioned to Shannon's father that he brought the drive. He handed it to him, reiterating what he did on it, and suggested that after dinner they go through it together. Her father thanked him sincerely and agreed, and then the conversation continued on.

Only a few moments later, Shannon's mother asked both of them if the company John worked for could possibly help with the final execution of their renovation. Shannon promptly said that John had already set up the plans and could get them a substantial discount on it all as well. John discreetly and softly nudged Shannon's leg under the table without looking at her, quickly speaking up and saying how he still needed to get all the approvals worked out first but was hopeful that it should be fine. Her parents were very happy to hear it and said they understood if it didn't work, either way.

Later that night, on the drive home, John said to Shannon, "Why did you answer that question about my company?" asking in a flippant way that made it clear he wasn't really looking for an answer. He knew it wasn't that big of a deal, and the approvals were almost certainly going to be fine, but he still didn't want her parents to know before he was sure, and he knew Shannon knew that.

Shannon, now rather exhausted from the day, replied, "It obviously slipped. I didn't mean to."

John, now also exhausted, kind of snapped back at her response, "I understand it was a mistake, but I don't understand how you could make it."

They went back and forth for a little while, each possessing less energy now than earlier, yet somehow arguing with more intensity. At some point, it became unnecessarily personal, and each said things that left bruises on the other's mind. It didn't take long before they both more or less nonverbally agreed that they had said enough. The rest of the car ride was mostly quiet.

Upon getting home, the two continued to mostly pout around and avoid each other. They watched some TV and then went to bed without saying much more than a couple words, each falling asleep with a sour taste in their mouth, both wanting to just turn around and wash it out with apologies and amends, but neither doing so.

This is the 658th time John has lived this day. At least once every week, he relives this or one of the prior several days through memory-retrieval software. The software works by using a brain-computer interface, which scans the short- and long-term memory areas of the user's brain, retrieving, mapping, and reconstructing their neural firings as the user attempts to recall specific memories. Simultaneously, it scans and maps the visual network part of the brain that is activated in relation to the memories, conjoining the two sources of data and forming it into a hyper-real, filmlike, interpretational rendering, which can be saved like a video and experienced as a POV through VR and AR devices.

This particular day, this particular memory, was the last one John had with Shannon. The next morning, on her walk to work, while stepping out into an intersection she crossed nearly every day, a driver, running a red light at near-full speed, hit Shannon, throwing her into the air and sprawling her across the street. When ambulances arrived on the scene, they were only able to confirm that she was dead.

This last day that he had with her, and a collection of some several other days prior, were the only clear, full days John could properly retrieve following the accident. Now, he occasionally alternates across the different days, which are mostly essentially the same, and sometimes watches just individual moments that he was able to recall as isolated memories, but something about this last full day specifically feels the clearest and most real. He loves re-experiencing it as if it were his actual day, just to hear Shannon's voice, see her face, and experience the illusion of being there with her for the last time. Every time, however, he has to watch himself treat Shannon with crassness, impatience, and disregard over what was now so clearly nothing. Generally simple, insignificant blips of order and plans, almost always a mistake that was equal part, if not fully his own, almost always things with the consequence of little to nothing; generally minor inconveniences turned major; generally good moments or days turned bad for no real reason. And every time, it devastates him. But despite these days being filled with mundane ordinariness and these childish displays of useless anger and frustration, they were better than almost all the days John has had since.

People often say, "Live every day as if it were your last." But far less commonly do you hear, "Live every day as if it were everyone else's last." It isn't easy for John. It's a constant effort. The loss of his wife didn't make obvious but nearly impossible clichés of life any easier. For a while, it made even just showering feel like a hike. But as a token to the lesson of her memory, John now tries with full commitment to consider in each and every interaction he has with those he likes, loves, or hates: what if this were his last one? What if yesterday's was or tomorrow's will be?

One never knows for sure which memory will be their last with someone until they can't form any anymore. And now, every time John goes out into the world with friends, family, or strangers, he tries to remind himself and ask, "If this were the last time, the memory that I would have to relive over and over as the last one, would it hurt to watch more than it has to?"

"Everything Happens for a Reason" (Until It Doesn't)

I did everything right. I worked hard. I played according to the rules. I was kind as often as anyone can be. I led a good, decent life. Why then am I lying here in a hospital bed with my house destroyed and my life on the edge of being a life anymore?

I was with my wife in our brand-new home. After I had recently been promoted at my job, we moved from a rougher neighboring city. Our new house was beautiful and in a perfect neighborhood. We had worked so hard for it, and things were really starting to go quite well for us. Life was at a high point, and I had finally seemed to pull all the pieces together. Then, in an instant, in the most literal sense, the world crumbled beneath me, and my life came crashing down on top of me.

Earthquakes are a fairly common occurrence where we live, but most go unfelt, and the rare ones that are felt are typically nothing.

We were eating dinner when we felt one hit. We covered under the kitchen table, just in case. We waited there for a little while, even after the tremor seemed to subside. Then we returned to our dinner. Then, several minutes later, the real one hit. The first turned out to just be the foreshock. A 2.9 suddenly became a 6. Our house folded in on itself, and I was struck with falling sections of the kitchen window. One of them knocked me unconscious, and the other punctured my abdomen. Next thing I know, I am here in a hospital bed.

Fortunately, my wife came out fairly unharmed, suffering only a few minor injuries. The doctors discovered that my injury lacerated my liver, though, and caused internal bleeding. They performed emergency surgery upon my arrival.

Once inside, though, they apparently discovered that it was worse than they thought. They tried stopping the bleeding but seemed to have only been able to temporarily slow it down. The doctor said I might still survive, but probably not. They're going to run a few more tests and see if it makes sense to try another surgery. And so, I lie here. Waiting. Thinking about how, throughout my whole life, I had basically always believed that there was a reason for everything that happened to me or because of me. Everything was always a part of some sequence of reasoning and explanations. I always felt like the things that happened to me were a part of some bigger picture of me. And the things that happened because of me were mostly correlated with my efforts and abilities or lack thereof. However, when I awoke in the hospital and slowly began to realize the circumstances of my current condition, naturally, I searched for the reason. The explanation for why this happened to me and what good it could possibly be for. And after trying as hard as I could, I have found nothing.

Many of my friends and family who rushed to the hospital upon hearing the news have tried to console me and offer their own insights and explanations. Some said it was God's will. Some said it was my destiny, as if it was a good thing. Some said that everything would be okay and that there is always a reason in the universe, even if we don't see or understand it. I wanted to believe them, but I couldn't. As I've thought more and more about it, I've realized that every reason or explanation they gave me was merely a result of their own need for a reason, paired with their inability to find any. They were all efforts to find an exemption from conceding to the truth—that there was no good reason. At least none that had anything to do with me.

Saying it was a god, or the universe's specific plan for me, or whatever else, were all but feeble attempts to claim that there must be a good, just reason despite the fact that there were none in sight. The Earth's crust moves, and because of this, some rock broke underground, and then the ground shook. That's the reason. And perhaps that's a good reason for the Earth. But certainly not for me, who by chance was on top of it in the wrong place at the wrong time. That part has no reason, other than the reason of chance, which is no good reason.

I wonder, then, as I lie here dying in this seemingly reasonless way, what this conclusion means about all the other reasons I thought things happened for. If, to my knowledge, I've never done anything deserving of such a tragedy, how then could there be any good reason for this event occurring onto me? And if there is no good reason for this event, how then could there be any good reason for any event that led me to this one?

I lie here looking back at my life, trying to make sense of everything, and I realize something foolishly obvious I somehow overlooked. Every time I said, "Everything happens for a reason." Every time I heard it and believed it, every time I seemingly found a reason for why something happened to me, I never meant that it happened for a bad reason. I meant that it happened for a good reason—a just reason. I meant that there was some considerate order to the universe, and everything in my story was placed there to allow me to become the winner of it. But how foolish was I to think this—that I was somehow special, somehow important? And that somehow the universe agreed and gave me immunity from the fact that no one wins this thing.

Of course, I've always known that fortune and tragedy pass no judgment or prejudice on who they touch. There is a history of tragedies caused onto good people and fortunes caused onto bad people as proof. And yet, I lived and thought as if I was somehow exempt from what this meant.

Perhaps there are others who suffered from this same earthquake who will live on to give it good reasons. Maybe they will make greater connections with their neighbors and community. Maybe it will inspire them to make great changes in their lives. Maybe they will rebuild their homes into something nicer that they've always wanted. Maybe some will even attribute their own good reasons to my early death, and so on. But no one's reasons will be mine. For me, and those incapable of finding any, it will have none.

I wonder then, who is right? Those who claim that something happened for a good reason or those who don't find any in the same event? I wonder if perhaps both are right simultaneously.

Even with everything I've said, I still believe everything in my life had a reason. Not because it had one, but because I gave it one. Because as long as I was still living and observing and reacting, I could give what happened to me or because of me a reason for happening. And in this sense, I was not entirely wrong when I said things happened for a reason. But I was certainly not entirely right either. I was right in creating reasons, in feeling them. But I was wrong in thinking they were real, that they were anything beyond what I created for myself to help me through it all. In truth, the events of our lives don't need reasons. We need them.

When my wife tells me it's going to be okay, she doesn't know. But she hopes. And I can't blame her for this. It's a curious but truly human and respectable act—to hope. And I think I did the same thing every time I thought or felt that anything happened for a reason. I was simply hoping it did, hoping that everything could make sense and that it would be okay.

I think, in this, everything that seems to happen for a reason is not proof that anything happens for a reason, but proof of hope—proof that one is still around observing, interpreting, and working to give things a reason out of the resilience and cleverness of the human spirit. But I realize now that at some point for us all, the pen with which we write our reasons will dry up. And when this moment comes, there will be no ink left to write a reason for running out of ink. And so, until then, I say I will lie here writing in this hospital bed, revolting against the hopelessness, creating every last reason I can.

The Great Divide – What Lies Beyond Our Perception?

L ying on her bed horizontally, her chin propped up on one of her pillows, Rebecca watched her fish swim around its tank, moving from the right side to the left side, pausing there for a moment, then from the left to the right, pausing there for a moment, and then back, over and over, as it usually did. While watching her fish, whom she had named Shiny, Rebecca talked about her day and whatever else was on her mind, as she usually did.

Rebecca was a very intelligent young child. And perhaps somewhat related to this, she was also quite a lonely, isolated child. She had bad social anxiety as a consequence of her genetics, her tendency to overthink, and parents who also suffered from various social anxieties, surrounding Rebecca with a constant, unsettling tension during her formative years. As a result, Rebecca often had a difficult time communicating, especially with kids her own age, and struggled to make many friends during this early part of her life.

In a sort of way, at this time, her best friend was her fish. Some of the greatest conversations she ever had were with Shiny. She would tell it everything, unhindered and unencumbered. She would complain to Shiny about her parents and teachers. She would tell it what she was sad about when she was sad, what she was happy about when she was happy, what she wanted to do, who she wanted to be when she was older, and so on. All the while, Shiny swam its few routes back and forth, every once in a while stopping and staring with its naïve, unaware eyes back in her direction. Still at an inevitably naïve age, Rebecca felt the inclination to believe that, in these moments, Shiny understood and personally loved her like a friend. Although it's possible that Shiny did, at some point, start to recognize the recurring patterns of Rebecca's facial arrangement and associate her likeness with food, it of course did not actually like or know Rebecca in any real sense of these terms at all. It was a fish. It hadn't the slightest clue as to how to form the slightest clue of what, or in this case who, Rebecca was. Its mental framework far too small; its perceptual and cognitive capacity essentially null.

Shiny would go on to live twelve healthy years, aging with Rebecca through her adolescence. Out of habit, Rebecca continued to talk with Shiny throughout the rest of its life. Of course, Rebecca would soon realize how foolish it was to be talking with her fish, understanding that Shiny almost certainly did not get her or like her on any level at all. But nonetheless, she still enjoyed the routine. On the occasions when Shiny's eyes looked back at her, Rebecca found herself wondering, instead, that if not really her, what exactly was Shiny experiencing? Could it recognize her in any form at all? Could it understand her at all? Did it really process anything as the reality that was actually happening? Rebecca reflected on the fact that Shiny obviously knew she was some sort of something that was happening around or to it whenever she did something like feed it or put her hand into the tank, yet, at the same time, since Shiny did not and could not know what that something actually was and why it was doing what it was doing, Rebecca's image and touch and vocal vibrations were things happening to it with no conscious source. There was no way for it to understand that Rebecca was a living human being that loved it, that cared for it; that those sound waves she emitted had meaning contained inside them, that there even were sound waves at all; that there was specific, thoughtful, conscious intention in the movements around and toward it.

Although Shiny could never know, it had a huge impact on Rebecca's life, their sort-of relationship greatly influencing her as she asked these sorts of questions, learning more about herself and her interests in the world.

Between the bond she formed with Shiny, her social anxiety, and her hard time communicating, over the course of her early teens, Rebecca became deeply interested in the ways in which species develop and carry out language, delving further into this research field known as linguistics.

In high school, Rebecca created and ran her school's first linguistics club, took multiple summer linguistics courses hosted by local universities, and explored deeper and deeper into her own research. In college, she worked for several linguistic and cognitive science research groups, was an assistant for the school's leading anthropological linguistics professor, and already began concluding her senior thesis by this time, garnering serious interest and respect from her professor as well as other faculty. By age twenty-two, Rebecca received her PhD, and by her early thirties, she had become a leading linguist, teaching at UC Berkley, writing several very successful books, winning numerous awards, and becoming internationally recognized for her work in language acquisition and psycholinguistics.

At age forty-five, however, Rebecca's career would dramatically shift, diverting her in a totally different direction. Earlier this same year, a strange radio signal was intercepted by a telescope that was used as part of a university program that scanned deep space searching for signs of extraterrestrial intelligent life. This was the first time in human history that an observed space signal showed sufficient power, suitably narrow bandwidth, and a range of small radio frequencies that added up to indicate an artificial nature to the signal. Upon examination, it was believed to be a highly likely candidate for extraterrestrial life.

As a result of this groundbreaking moment, efforts to decipher and analyze the signal, develop the search for subsequent signals, and transmit corresponding signals back into space all increased. As a part of this growing initiative, Rebecca was sought out and recruited by an organization known as the International Contact Group for Extraterrestrial Intelligence, the hope being to utilize her leading knowledge of language acquisition and language types for the purposes of both interpreting and broadcasting messages to and from alternate types of beings. Rebecca couldn't turn down such an unusual and interesting opportunity, and so, after a little negotiating, she took the job.

Years and years went by. Rebecca became a key member of the organization, leading a specific team that worked on developing and broadcasting various sorts of signals into deep space. Additionally, they developed and sent out space probes housing various plaques, audio and video recordings, music, mathematics, and other forms of information and communication. Despite these great efforts, though, no explanation would ever conclusively be found for the initial signal, and no more of its kind would ever seem to reappear.

Throughout this later portion of her career, Rebecca couldn't help but wonder more and more where everybody was. In a potentially endless space with billions and billions of years behind humanity, how was there no one else out there? Almost every night, Rebecca spent some time on her porch looking up into the stars, entirely perplexed by the strange paradox that her work seemed to illuminate and reinforce. Somehow it is likely that at least several hundred million, if not several billion Earth-sized planets with inhabitable conditions for life were out there in just the Milky Way galaxy alone. And potentially trillions of habitable planets in the universe at large. And if human development and technology were to be extrapolated to any reasonable degree, in relation to the size and age of the universe, even if just a small percentage of these planets had formed life, the galaxy should be rife with signs of it by now. Yet, the universe appeared dead and quiet. Humanity, alone. The Great Silence.

Right now, Rebecca continues on. She moves around her planet, mostly back and forth between two sections, work and home, pausing and hovering in one for a little, then to the other, hovering there for a little, and then back again, over and over, as she usually does.

Right now, as it usually does, a being from the species known as what loosely translates into 01100111 01101111 01100100 01110011 00100000 00100000, named what loosely translates into 01101100 01100001 01101110 01101001 01100001 01101011 01100101 01100001 00100000 00100000, or just 011-L for short, hovers outside (or sort of in between) time and space, watching Rebecca, talking to her about whatever is on its *mind*.

011-L is a member of a super-intelligent species who, a long, long time ago, evolved from one of the earliest lineages of life that formed and survived the early budding universe. As it successfully evolved through time, it developed intelligence, built technology, extended out past its host planet, harnessed the power of its host star, eventually breached the bonds of biological and neurobiological conditions, built and collectivized with other galactic lifeforms, and finally, harnessed the total energy of its host galaxy. Over time, the super-intelligent species had gotten smaller and smaller, moving further up the interdimensional rungs of physical reality until it became what would appear immaterial to all beings of other dimensional levels. Now, the species traverses the universe, exploring and perceiving things outside and in between time, not confined to it or to the same physical material and conditions that confine one-, two-, three-, four-, five-, six-, seven-, eight-, and nine-dimensional space.

Rebecca's reality is accessible to 011-L in a way that might be similar to the way Rebecca accesses information from an external computer hard drive, displaying the stored information bits onto a separate monitor screen. Accessible to species with the technology to locate, extract, and read it, her reality's information is contained in bits of information stored on the outer edge of the universe's geometric surface, which can then be observed through a kind of holographic projection. Although this is metaphorically sound, in truth, trying to accurately explain and understand such a phenomenon with these words through such a human mode of thinking would be like Rebecca trying to explain physics to her fish.

Specifically, 011-L is an especially intelligent super-intelligent being. Perhaps somewhat related to this, it is also a particularly lonely and isolated super-intelligent being. It has a bad form of what could sort of be the equivalent to social anxiety as a consequence of its tendency to overthink and some portion its maladaptive hereditary input codes. Consequently, it often has a difficult time communicating with others, especially its own kind. It has and continues to struggle to make many friends, and in a way, at this time, Rebecca is its best friend. Some of the greatest conversations it has ever had were with Rebecca. It tells her everything, unhindered and unencumbered. It complains to her. It tells her about its life, about what it's like to be alone and to exist in the condition that it does, what its favorite and least favorite things are, its favorite places in the universe, and so on.

Early on, when 011-L, by chance, picked out Rebecca, not too dissimilar from the way in which Rebecca picked out Shiny, it initially thought that she understood and loved it like a friend. That when she stopped and looked up into the stars with her naïve, unaware eyes pointed in its direction, she knew 011-L. But of course, it didn't take long for 011-L to realize that there was no way for Rebecca to understand and know of it at all. She was a human. She hadn't the slightest clue as to how to form the slightest clue of what, or in this case who, 011-L was. She couldn't know that it loved her, that it cared for her, that the interdimensional frequencies it emitted had meaning contained inside them, that there even were any frequencies at all, that there could be intention in the universe's motion around her.

Rebecca could visually see and feel the oscillations of physical material that were the consequences of 011-L's thoughts and actions, manifesting at the quantum level in what appeared to be random particle behavior, but she could not know nor attribute any thoughts or concepts to this. To Rebecca and the rest of humanity, there was no real source. Her mental framework was far too small; her perceptual and cognitive capacity essentially null in comparison.

Ironically, 011-L and the rest of its species never knew that Rebecca and her human colleagues had been trying to contact them or anyone. The physical objects sent out looked like meaningless debris, and the radio signals, on the few occasions that they actually reached them, appeared to be just a primitive, foreign noise that translated into nothing for them. At times, some did consider the possibility that the radio broadcasts were some form of an effort to communicate with them, but just like how Rebecca did not seriously bark back at a dog when it was barking at her to communicate, this species never thought to or knew how to properly bark back. Except for one time when they tried in a kind of humorous, playful effort, which ultimately served no purpose.

In truth, there was a galaxy rife with technology and signs of other life. Rebecca and the rest of her species were right in this conclusion but wrong when they assumed that they would recognize it. And so, continuing to this day, they still think they're alone. Like most species similar to them, they don't see anything, and so, they assume nothing is there. But just as Rebecca was right there in the room with Shiny, but Shiny had no way of knowing that the physical shape of her was an intelligent being named Rebecca, right there in the room with Rebecca was 011-L, but Rebecca had no way of knowing that the emergent physical phenomena of it was a super intelligent being named 011-L.

Dying – A Guided Experience

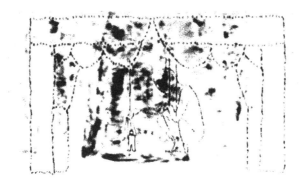

I don't know how many times I had heard, or at least observed some form of the idea, that classic overused cliché that one's whole life flashes before their eyes in the conscious moments right before dying. I had heard it a lot. I know that. I had even heard it used in plenty of non-death-related instances when people just wanted to add a little grandiosity to a situation or story. I myself had probably even used it in a story or two. It is, of course, one of those things that doesn't really make much sense while you're alive, though. After all, how could one's entire life flash before their eyes? Presumably, the use of the word *eyes* here is meant to represent sort of the visualization center of the mind, as opposed to literally the eyeballs, but even still, how could the mind speed up years' worth of experiences so fast that it could all be perceived and recollected in minutes or even seconds, and still be discernable? I had always wondered at the absurdity of the notion whenever it was mentioned or represented in something. Now, in this moment, on the side of the road, contorted and lacerated, I was about to find out exactly what it meant.

I didn't know exactly how much blood the human body could lose before dying, but it didn't take long for me to realize that I was getting pretty close. I could feel my body shutting down, and I started experiencing weird pains that didn't hurt so much as confused and nauseated me. Harder to describe than it was to feel. I could also hear that people were saying things to me that were indicative of someone dying. Things like, "Please don't close your eyes. Just hold on a little bit longer. It's going to be okay. An ambulance is on the way." Stuff like that, but with different words and in a much more pleading, dramatic tone. They all knew as well as I did, though, what was happening and that no amount of force of will to keep my eyes open was going to outmatch death, if it were to come. At this point, it felt much better to just close my eyes anyway. It somehow relieved the pain a little. I accepted that I was dying by this point. It wasn't even really a conscious choice. My body knew. My mind knew.

After this moment of acceptance, my mind certainly did race at a sort of flash-like speed. But mostly, it felt comparable to that of what I would imagine a lucid panic attack feels like on twenty cups of coffee. I didn't see everything from my life, and there was no apparent rhyme or reason or order to what I did. I did, however, feel a great sense of regret as I ruminated across all the feelings and thoughts and memories that appeared. I thought about who I would never see again and what I would never do again. I thought about how I wouldn't see what colors were going to be in the next evening's sunset, how I would never brush my teeth again, how I would never feel the air running over my skin or flowing into my nose again. I thought about the low hum of all the appliances in my house that I would never hear again.

Then I thought about what I never saw or did but always wanted to—all the times I never told people how I felt or how much I cared about them, all the opportunities I let go because I was scared, all the habits and problems in my life that I always wanted to change but never did. Then I thought about how much time I wasted worrying about these things, the time I wasted hating myself, the time I wasted being unhappy, and the time I wasted getting mad at myself for being unhappy, when I should have been happy. I thought about how I rarely ever fully synced up with what I knew I should have done or how I should have thought, how I seemed to always deceive or sabotage myself in the process. I would get close to the ideal or sublime that I always knew existed in each moment, but then I would run the other way.

However upsetting and sad this whole part was, it kind of fit my Hollywood expectations of dying, which only added to the disappointment. It was anticlimactic, like predicting the end of a movie. Now, I found myself getting upset and angry about the disappointingly rational and predictable process of getting upset, angry, and regretful while dying. Even here, I was literally regretting my final moments of life, as they occurred. How foolish could I be? What kind of being hates itself or brings suffering onto itself, knowing that hating itself and suffering makes them miserable? What kind of being spends their final moments alive being miserable about their life?

In this ridiculous, self-loathing rumination, as if coerced by something that was predetermined to happen at a certain moment of the body and brain turning off, a sudden pause occurred. A pause that felt much more like a flash than the previous flash that was occurring. It was not a flash of speed, but a sudden flash of ceasing speed. Like a camera flash to a little rodent, it stunned me and stopped everything.

As if my consciousness had finally surrendered, told by my subconscious that there was no self or life left to defend, for the first time, I felt free. Not free in the sense that I was able to do whatever I wanted. Quite the opposite. Free in the sense that in only a few moments, I literally would not be able to do anything I wanted. In this, I suddenly became so completely indifferent to everything that everything became clear. I saw myself through an entirely different lens, as if a smudge on my preexisting lens had been cleared off, revealing what had always been obstructed from me.

I continued thinking for a little while, but my thinking was different. It wasn't critical, rational, or judgmental. For the first time in my entire life, I saw who I really was.

While alive, I understood that I had a conscious brain and an unconscious brain. I had learned about these rudimentary psychology concepts as a young child and considered the implications of them frequently throughout my life. However, these terms never really translated in any practical or helpful way, at least not for me. If anything, they only made me feel like I had two parts of my brain, the part that was me and the part that wasn't. I was, of course, my conscious brain, and my unconscious brain was something else that I was constantly fighting or trying to conquer. This wasn't wrong, per se, but it wasn't exactly right either. At a minimum, it certainly wasn't helpful. It took being mangled on the side of a road with parts of my brain seemingly being turned off to actually understand it.

Sure, I was never my unconscious brain, but I was never my conscious brain either, just like I was never my heart, or my hand, or anything else on its own. I was never even solely what was contained inside my body. I was everything, in and out. I was the puppet and the puppeteer, the puppeteer being sort of my unconscious brain, but also much more than my unconscious brain. It was what made and fueled my unconscious brain, what made my brain as whole, what made everything.

Admittedly, while alive, this might have sounded confusing or pretentiously cheesy or like spiritual nonsense or even cliché if someone had told me. Perhaps it is to you right now. Most things about life while I was alive, though, sounded confusing, pretentiously cheesy, or like spiritual nonsense. However, after a certain point of being viscerally aware of your approaching mortality, you don't think about things like that anymore. You stop putting this filter of judgment on top of sincerity or cliched archetypal experiences. Regardless, even if you are not in this same state, if you can humor me just for a moment, imagine the puppet and puppeteer I referred to. Consider how a puppeteer is only a puppeteer if it has and manipulates a puppet. If there were no such thing as a puppet, there would be no such thing as a puppeteer, and vice versa. The puppet is not the puppeteer, and the puppeteer is not the puppet, but without the other, each ceases to exist in the contexts of their definitions.

I spent my whole life thinking I was the puppet contained by the strings, the consciousness contained by the brain, the brain contained by the body, the body contained by the world. And as a result,

I spent my whole life at war against everything I felt contained by. I spent my life pulling at the strings, trying to rip myself from them. These strings, and my pulling at them, however, was the source of all the self-sabotage and self-loathing, all the divisions and limits between what I wanted for myself and what I never could have. I was contained by strings, and furthermore, I added constant tension to them be pulling at them, making things worse by always trying to make things better.

A little earlier, I would have been gravely regretful of this realization. Far more than my earlier regrets. I would have tormented over the idea that I ruined my life, missing the entire point, making things worse than they had to be. However, I did not get mad or regretful at all. By this point, my conscious sense of self had fully given up on defending itself. I didn't care. I recognized that I had no choice in these strings existing in the first place. They were written in my DNA. They were written in the DNA of my DNA. And furthermore, I had no choice in pulling at them either. If I was both the puppet and puppeteer, even the act of pulling on these strings and struggling toward something was, in fact, part of the whole show. My being came with strings, and my being came with a desire to pull at the strings. So, what was I to do other than to live with strings and pull at them?

I spent my whole life fighting who I was, often hating who I was, trying to be happier or better or something. Sometimes I would be successful, but even then, I would mostly just return to the same starting point, beginning the fight all over again. But of course, this was because I never was who I thought I was. This part of myself that I always thought I was in a fight with, turns out, it was actually more of a dance. And without the constant push and pull, without the struggle, without seemingly having missed the point, there would have been no point at all. No dance. No show.

The things I could've changed, I did; the things I couldn't, I didn't; and the things I didn't know I should've, I never even thought to try. I was exactly who I could have been, exactly who I needed to be. I did everything right by doing a great deal of things wrong. There was nothing to regret. Regret implies that I chose how things went, but I never really had a choice at all. I didn't choose who I was any more or any less than anything else that is, was, or ever will be—no more than a dog chooses to be a dog or a rock chooses to be a rock. I just woke up and was. I didn't choose who my parents were, what my brain was like, what my body was like, what my first sight was, my first conscious experience, my anxieties, my fears, or any of what these things caused me to do. Now, I was about to fall asleep forever, in the last choice I never made, holding the thing that I had been chasing my whole life.

What had been the source of my misery was now, in the final moment, the source of my bliss. The source of my self- discovery. My acceptance of who I really was while alive and who I am now while dead.

Who Am I? – The Mysterious Thing You Always Are

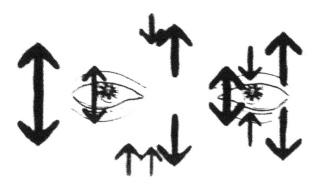

The year was 2122. Humanity had recently begun its first real phase of mass-scale bionic body augmentations. For the first time, it was now normal for people to swap out body parts with more robust, technologically integrated prosthetics for non-medical purposes. A man named Jack, age twenty-nine, had held off on all body modifications for as long as he could and was of the small remaining percentage of entirely organic adult human bodies. Jack worked one of the few still-existing physical-labor-based jobs, assisting in the construction, upkeep, and use of robotic machinery used to load and unload cargo shipping containers onto commercial ships that self-navigated themselves to and from delivery ports.

Being one of the few remaining workers with biological arms and legs, Jack had inevitably fallen behind the increasingly high standards of the job. Naturally, his biological arms and legs grew tired and could exert only about one-fifteenth the force of the vast majority of his coworkers who had opted for the company-funded CyberBuild brand mechanical prosthetic arms and legs.

In order to stay afloat in the competitive, automated job market, on June 3, 2124, Jack finally opted in to giving up his biological arms and legs for bionic replacements. These bionic prosthetics were powered through various electrodes that were implanted in areas of the brain that control movement and process touch sensation. The electrodes were then activated and engaged by the user's brain neurons as the user thought about and sensed movement, directing nerve signals back through the electrodes and into the bionic limbs, moving them essentially just like biological arms and legs.

Following the procedure, at the bionic surgery facility, Jack filled out all the necessary forms with his new hands. It was a bit tricky, but not too bad. At the bottom of the form, he signed his name on the signature line: Jack Outis.

Several years went by. It took Jack a little time to fully adapt and get used to the idea of his new arms and legs, but soon enough, he came to barely even notice them. Initially, he didn't recognize them when he looked down, but since he never really considered his arms and legs to be a crucial part of his identity, it was relatively easy to eventually just assimilate them as a part of him.

Simultaneous to Jack getting fully accustomed to the new appendages, with technology and medical advancements seeming to only continue to multiply, much of the rest of humanity had begun taking on other newly developed, more extreme bionic augmentations in order to keep up with the increasingly competitive, automated job market, as well as the heightening standards of living.

Over the span of about fifteen years, by age forty-five, Jack had exchanged out his rib cage, spine, eyes, ears, teeth, heart, several other organs, and eventually his skull and neck. The augmented replacements provided technological integrations that synchronized with external devices while also improving bodily strength, functionality, and longevity. These modifications were also intended to aid in slowing down the aging process and extending the universal average lifespan, which, with many of these initial bionic replacements, was predicted to easily extend past two or three hundred years at least. At this point, Jack was essentially a human brain in a vat atop an almost entirely different mechanical body.

The riskiest procedure, which also happened to be the last one

Jack underwent, was the skull replacement that changed out his normal skull for a bionicly integrated metal one, requiring his brain to be removed and then placed back into the new head, neck, and spinal configuration. From the exterior, the skull looked like a completely normal human head with otherwise natural-looking skin and facial features, making the aesthetic transition fairly benign. However, each person who underwent the procedure was given the choice to change how their face looked to essentially anything they'd like, which Jack opted for. Never having really liked his face all that much, he decided on a new one that looked completely different.

Prior to and following the procedure, along with all the earlier procedures, Jack filled out and agreed to a variety of lengthy waiver and clearance forms, signing his name on each: Jack Outis.

Within only a year of each procedure, sometimes just a few months, Jack mostly became used to his new augmented body parts. The face was, of course, the hardest and longest one to adapt to, but eventually, within the year or so, he started to recognize himself in it, just the same as his old one. His face was never really him anyway, Jack felt. It was merely just the cover in front of him, and any arrangement or form of it could be him just as easily—at least once he got used to it. Ultimately, he lived contently with his new bionic body, feeling like just a physically improved version of his original self.

Several more years went by. By this point, as a result of increasing artificial intelligence development, Jack had been automated out of his original job field, and the global socioeconomic system had shifted away from nearly all physical- based jobs. Consequently, after a harsh transition period, new industries, markets, and jobs started to take form across the internet landscape, especially related to things like VR, AR, art, communication, experiential services, software, and so on. Jack eventually landed a job as a set designer and coder for virtual reality entertainment performances. As a result of this shift, the long-anticipated mass-market consumer application of implantable brain–machine interfaces was approved during this time in the year 2146.

A company called Neuratie led the charge, beginning their first consumer-market rollout with their Model B-I brain-machine interface. Like all brain-machine interfaces, it worked by implanting tiny chips into the bionic or organic skull of the user. Tiny wires would then be connected from these chips and spread out into various essential parts of the brain. The wires could then receive and send messages from and through the user's neurons. As a result, the user could connect their brain to the cloud and, via brainwaves alone, operate devices and bionic technologies, communicate nonverbally with others online, as well as share and access public information, essentially merging thought with internet and wearable technology. One of the most notable features of the interface was that it allowed users to select technical skills and aptitudes that could be downloaded directly into the brain as if they had been learned throughout a lifetime, or delete skills as if they had been forgotten, in just a matter of seconds. By activating patterns and sequences of nerve impulses, the technology rendered specific body movements and mental abilities that carried out various skills.

Like all prior augmentations, the brain-machine interface was fully optional. Every step of the way, including this one, one was faced with the choice to either augment or not. However, inevitably, most (if not all) conceded eventually, due to the apparent will to live that technology possessed and carried out through human socialization.

For many years, recreational brain-machine interfaces were met with especially high resistance by groups that were against the general consumer adoption of the technology. For many prior decades, the technology had been exclusively approved and used for medical purposes only, strictly assisting with neurological disorders and body paralysis. Now, however, because of the need for enhanced mental capacities and digital integrations, the technology was approved and set to be used more or less to modify otherwise "healthy" human brains.

Jack was one of the many who initially opposed it. It was one thing to relinquish parts or even the full body, but to go into the more abstract parts of the brain was something else entirely. However, just like all the prior augmentations, the technology exponentially crept into the norm as more and more individuals adopted it, creating a greater sense of ostracism and exclusion toward those who did not. As with most things like it, it reached its inevitable tipping point and went from abnormal to have one to abnormal not to.

Eventually, Jack underwent the simple, essentially painless procedure and awoke into a new technologically integrated brain. After going through a brief moment of recovery, he turned on the interface, viewing it through his augmented eyes. He mentally filled in his name on the startup screen: Jack Outis. It was weird at first, but mentally deciding to write versus mentally deciding to write and then watching your arm do it were fundamentally no different, Jack found, and he took to it almost right away.

As time passed and Jack became more and more used to his newly modified brain, he downloaded and relinquished certain skills and aptitudes. After a certain point, to Jack's relief, it became clear that fundamentally there wasn't anything really changing about him—at least no more or less than just learning new skills. Throughout Jack's biological life, he had obviously learned and forgotten many skills, ideas, and capacities, but he still always felt like the same person. And here too, despite the extreme rate, the same phenomenon seemed to occur. He realized he was never his technical skills or abilities, but rather, the person experiencing them.

As the modern world moved further into the digital-mental realm, new brain-machine interface companies and models came out, aggressively competing. Corporations started to more commonly generate and push software updates to consumers in an effort to keep their models at the forefront. Some of the software updates were relatively benign and were no more than bug fixes or additional skillset options or better integrations with bionic prosthetics. However, some software updates began to go further, dipping into desires, interests, and habits.

Users who moved forward with these updates could do things like increase or decrease tendencies toward certain states, remove undesirable desires, and download or delete interests. Naturally, these software updates were again met with reluctance by many. Jack, along with plenty of others like him, avoided any updates that altered more than just the existing functionality for as long as possible.

Jack felt strongly that the alterations of tendencies or desires or interests would change his entire sense of self-identity and render him unfamiliar to himself. However, as time passed and the same pattern of history unfolded, Jack, along with the majority of others like him, eventually opted in and downloaded some of these software updates.

In the year 2153, Jack downloaded his first major software update known as Version Prime, an update that allowed users to control and self-regulate personal desires, habits, and interests. Upon the download, as usual, Jack had to read the terms of service and digitally sign his name where asked. He signed: Jack Outis.

Following the software update, through essentially no more than a push of a button, Jack could and did download and delete desires, interests, and daily routines, often relinquishing old ones to make room for the new. Across Jack's entire lifetime, prior to the NeuraTie brain interface, he experienced many different interests, desires, habits, and life routines, and never felt like a different person. Even if one desire or interest led to another, the transitional period between them always kept him feeling like him. Although more extreme, the software updates seemed to feel no different. Since Jack was still always the one choosing to download or delete these features of himself, it all still felt like it was based off of his foundational desire for certain desires, interests, and routines, strung along a consistent, unbroken line of self- identity.

And so, even though Jack had an almost completely different body, new set of technical skills, new desires and interests, and new daily life, at this point, in his mind, he still felt like Jack.

In the year 2157, Jack downloaded Software Update Version Senior: a brand-new, revolutionary update that allowed users to have memories added or removed from the memory storage part of their minds. Initially, this was intended to be used toward removing memories of trauma, but it eventually evolved into more general memory removal, as well as positive memory implantation. Users could now plant false memories inside their long-term memory, altering how they remembered the quality of their lives. Jack slowly participated in this, deleting traumatic memories about his former biological childhood self, as well as implanting nice memories throughout his teens and twenties to counterbalance the period of prolonged depression he actually lived through. These alterations were integrated subtly into the mind over time, so it felt like the original memories simply faded away and the new ones weren't even new—almost like how the biological mind might block out or repaint bad memories through repression or nostalgia.

At this point, Jack forgot, altered, and had false memories, different interests, desires, skills, opinions, and routines, and an almost completely different body. And yet, even across all of this, he continued to feel like Jack. It was as if as long as he still had a continuous memory of himself, he sustained a continuous tracking of himself, and thus, a consistent sense of self-identity—regardless of any change or accurate awareness of that change. He recognized that he was not the same person in any way and perhaps couldn't even know what that same person really was anymore, yet, somewhere in him, something still felt like him.

As part of the continual development and improvement of the technology, Jack filled out optional questionnaires about every month or so. At the top of each questionnaire form, it asked, "Please confirm your identity. Who are you?"

The Man Who Was Trapped Inside His Own Body

The strangest part was the realization. The moments when I first started gaining consciousness. It was surreal, to say the least. I had no idea what had happened or what was happening. It was an unfathomable, dreamlike disorientation and sense of helplessness that could only possibly be known through first-hand experience.

When I first came to awareness, I was lying on my bed with my face angled up, slightly to the left. I could see and think as if everything were normal, except one thing: I couldn't move. I couldn't move my eyeballs from their fixed position. I couldn't control my eyelids to open or close them on command. I couldn't voluntarily move my arms or legs or any part of my upper or lower body. I couldn't open or close my mouth to speak or scream. I couldn't do anything other than lie confined to my fixed position.

Admittedly, at first, I thought I was dead. I thought I was in some strange afterlife limbo, just peering out at the world from where I had died. But everything seemed too real, too normal. And after a little time went by, I realized that I kept waking in and out of everything, as if there was still a sleeping and waking brain inside *me*.

I considered that perhaps instead, I was experiencing sleep paralysis or a sequence of really strange lucid dreams. But I didn't remember going to bed, and it quickly felt beyond that too. If it was a dream, why was I continually returning to what felt like the same dream over and over, which was just the same relatively banal situation of being stuck on my bed? And furthermore, I could remember each previous dream in each following dream, which didn't feel very dreamlike.

Over what must have been some length of dipping and peaking in and out consciousness, I considered every sort of strange hallucinatory and psychological possibility for what was going on, but the flurry of momentary awareness made it impossible to maintain mental clarity long enough to really flesh out any thoughts. It was all mostly a blur, and I had no idea what was happening.

After some further length of time, which I cannot speak to how long, I started coming into the awareness that there were people around me. My parents and older sister and what appeared to be doctors, nurses, and other unfamiliar voices and faces. They were all looking at me, interacting with me, talking to me—intensely in many cases. Doctors appeared to be testing and probing me with various equipment and lights. They were all treating me as if I was there physically but not mentally, as if I couldn't understand them. But during the moments when I was awake and aware, I could basically hear, see, and understand everything as if it were happening normally. I just couldn't say or move or do anything back. I was completely trapped inside my body.

It was hard to fully make sense of what was happening for a while, but eventually, after experiencing longer periods of conscious alertness, I started to hear and make out more of what was being said and done, and I realized that the issue wasn't metaphysical at all. I wasn't dead or dreaming or anything of the sort. It was very physical and real.

At one point, I recall hearing what seemed to be a doctor talking to my parents, saying that she believed I was mentally gone without any real way of knowing if or when I might return. I remember she said something about how it was still unclear exactly what was hap-

190   *THE HIDDEN STORY OF EVERY PERSON*

pening and suggested that were still other things to be done, tests to be performed, and other doctors to be consulted.

One of the scariest parts of the entire thing was much further in, when I heard what seemed to be the ninth or tenth doctor, who was, according to all the previous doctors, supposed to be one of the leading experts in cases like mine, essentially say that he didn't know what was happening either—that there was really no way of knowing for sure what was happening or if there was any real consciousness taking place inside me, and thus, no way of effectively treating or understanding my condition with any certainty. I also heard him say that the condition almost surely came with a 100 percent fatality rate.

I could sense the utter and complete devastation in my parents and friends and family without even needing to see or hear them. I knew that they, like I, had no control over what was happening and felt an ironically similar form of despairing helplessness. I had so many things I wanted to say to help them better understand. I had never wanted anything more in my life than to tell them that I was there, that I was still inside my head, and that I still knew who they were, that things might still be okay. But I couldn't. I couldn't say any of the words, or reach out and touch them, or blink on command, or communicate in any meaningfully intentional way. Communication was helplessly disconnected from me. I think that's probably one of the hardest things anyone can deal with: wanting to say and do something to help those you love, and not being able to.

For a mind that wants things, for a mind that seems to define itself through its ability to cause and effect, will and react, it all comes down to control. But when you find yourself in a reality that you essentially have no control over, you are confronted with an insatiable, overwhelming, drowning sense of anger, frustration, and terror. The feeling of being aware of what's happening but not being able to understand why or do anything about it. That is what it all boils down to.

What was happening was no longer really the primary question or concern for me. I knew basically enough about what was happening. And so, the question became why and what now?

In general, I could never truly tell how much time was passing, nor can I recall now. I do remember a distinct turning point, though, a point that I believe my entire survival hinged on. It was when I heard my parents talking with one of the doctors or nurses or someone about whether or not they might consider a time at which they would take me off life support. I remember hoping with unquestionable intensity that they wouldn't. That they would just hold on a little longer. I wanted to scream out to them and tell them to wait and that I was still in there. And in this, I suddenly realized that I wanted to keep living. That despite my condition, despite the obvious misery and potential hopelessness, when presented with the possibility of having it all end, I preferred the potential horribleness of it all continuing over the idea of it all ending. I preferred living and seeing it through, even if I was helplessly stuck inside myself with no control, and even if there was no clear chance of whether or not it would get any better. I wanted life in any form I could have it.

Somewhere around and after this point, I made the ironically conscious choice to quiet my consciousness. Not to surrender, but more the opposite, if anything—to strategically conserve my conscious efforts away from what might ordinarily be conscious; the sort of heavy thinking, ruminating, and attempting to control, solve, or make sense of the situation, and instead, I decided to just live in it as long as I could as well as I could.

The line between consciously giving up and being consciously intentional with how little you use your consciousness is both absurdly subtle and abstractly impossible to translate, and I can't say with any certainty how well I accomplished any kind of ideal balance, and I'm not sure any ideal balance is even possible. To even consider the idea with such terms already undermines it. But for a lack of better terms, it's what I think I tried to do.

Ultimately, the problem was only compounded by my relentless yearning and struggling against it; a continual fighting and waiting and expecting for things to get better and gain control over a reality I had none over. Of course, that was the natural response, and there's no denying the unimaginable difficulty of the condition. But my constant efforts and expectations of it resolving didn't help. Rather, it only seemed to make things worse. I felt like I was stuck in the Chinese finger trap thing that my grandpa used to have and show me when I was a younger child; the thing where the harder you try to pull your finger out, the tighter it squeezes around it. The more I squirmed and yearned for control, the tighter things got. There was no escape and no resolution other than learning how to live without one, which I've learned that paradoxically, in its own way, is one.

Fundamentally, I had no real control over anything outside myself. But I did have control, or at least the sense of control, over my thoughts. I was still there. And I could still think and consider how to think. And if there was any hope, it was in this. It was in subverting my own thinking against itself, in focusing more of my attention on things that I could control that might help pass the time in a meaningful way, in trying to find things to be appreciative of and interested in, in examining the complexity, wonder, and depth of beauty of things in and around me, even in the simplest moments of apparent banal nothingness.

The trick, it seemed, was not wanting or depending on control, not wanting or depending on answers, not looking for or expecting anything, really. It was just observing and appreciating as best I could, as deeply as I could, and as often as I could—trying my best to just be okay with just being. And I think only because of that, I was able to survive. I was able to want to survive and continue, and I was, at times, able to be okay. And then, eventually, I awoke. Muscle by muscle. Cell by cell. I awoke.

Robert Pantano is the creator of the YouTube channel and production house known as Pursuit of Wonder, which covers similar topics of philosophy, science, and literature through short stories, guided experiences, video essays, and more.

Robert Pantano
youtube.com/pursuitofwonder
PursuitofWonder.com

Printed in Great Britain
by Amazon

86241934R00119